Christmas at Fairacre

BOOKS BY MISS READ

Novels

Village School * Village Diary * Storm in the Village
Thrush Green * Fresh from the Country
Winter in Thrush Green * Miss Clare Remembers
Over the Gate * The Market Square * Village Christmas
The Howards of Caxley * Fairacre Festival
News from Thrush Green * Emily Davis * Tyler's Row
The Christmas Mouse * Farther Afield
Battles at Thrush Green * No Holly for Miss Quinn
Village Affairs * Return to Thrush Green * The White Robin
Village Centenary * Gossip from Thrush Green
Affairs at Thrush Green * Summer at Fairacre
At Home in Thrush Green * The School at Thrush Green
Mrs Pringle * Friends at Thrush Green * Changes at Fairacre
Celebrations at Thrush Green * Farewell to Fairacre
Tales from a Village School * The Year at Thrush Green
A Peaceful Retirement

Anthology

Country Bunch * Miss Read's Christmas Book

Omnibuses

Chronicles of Fairacre * Life at Thrush Green
More Stories from Thrush Green
Further Chronicles of Fairacre * Christmas at Fairacre
Fairacre Roundabout * Tales from Thrush Green
Fairacre Affairs * Encounters at Thrush Green
The Caxley Chronicles * Farewell, Thrush Green
The Last Chronicle of Fairacre

Non-fiction

Miss Read's Country Cooking
Tiggy
The World of Thrush Green
Early Days
(comprising A Fortunate Grandchild & Time Remembered)

Miss Read

* * * *

CHRISTMAS
at FAIRACRE

COMPRISING

No Holly for Miss Quinn

Christmas at Fairacre School

The Christmas Mouse

Illustrated by J. S. Goodall

ORION

First published in this edition in 2005 by Orion,
an imprint of the Orion Publishing Group Ltd.

Originally published in the omnibus edition *Christmas at Fairacre*
by Michael Joseph 1991
and Penguin Books 1992

A CIP catalogue record for this book is available
from the British Library.

ISBN 0 75287 383 0

Typeset at The Spartan Press Ltd,
Lymington, Hants

Printed in Great Britain by Clays Ltd, St Ives plc

The Orion Publishing Group
Orion House
5 Upper Saint Martin's Lane
London, WC2H 9EA

www.orionbooks.co.uk

Contents

* * * *

Foreword by Miss Read

I am delighted to see this winter collection from my writings about the imaginary village of Fairacre and its surroundings.

Winter may not be everyone's favourite season, but of all the year's festivals Christmas takes pride of place, and has lost none of its magic. This, no doubt, is partly because we hark back to the excitements of childhood Christmases but also because we look forward to renewing friendships and to taking part in the foremost of the church's festivals.

But the fact that Christmas Day falls in the dreariest time of the year also highlights its impact. We are usually in the grip of winter's cold, early darkness, frost and snow, and all the ills that they bring. Doubly precious, therefore, are our domestic comforts – a blazing fire, sustaining food, the comfort of friends and, at the end of the day, a warm bed.

In this collection of my writings about winter you will find many of these things. The celebrations and adventures mostly take place in the imaginary village of Fairacre, especially the school, the nearby market town of Caxley, or in that neighbourhood. Outside, the winter landscape has a beauty of its own: bare branches against a clear sky, brilliant stars on a frosty night and perhaps a swathe of untouched snow. But these beauties are best when seen from the comfort of one's home, with a good fire crackling and the smell of crumpets toasting for tea.

That is the charm of the winter season, the contrast between the cold and the warmth, the light and the dark. I hope you will enjoy Christmas and the wintertime in the book before you.

Miss Read 1991

No Holly for Miss Quinn

For Betty and Alan
with love

CHAPTER ONE

If you take the road from the downland village of Fairacre to Beech Green, you will notice three things.

First, it is extremely pretty, with flower-studded banks or wide grass verges, clumps of trees, and a goodly amount of hawthorn hedging.

Second, it runs steadily downhill, which is not surprising as the valley of the river Cax lies about six miles southward.

Third, it loops and curls upon itself in the most snake-like manner, so that, if you are driving, it is necessary to negotiate the bends prudently, in third gear, and with all senses alert.

Because of the nature of the road then, a certain

attractive house, set back behind a high holly hedge, escapes the attention of the passer-by. Holly Lodge began modestly enough as a small cottage belonging to a farming family at Beech Green. No one knows the name of the builder, but it would have been some local man who used the materials to hand, the flints from the earth, the oak from the woods and the straw from the harvest fields, to fashion walls, beams and thatched roof. When the work was done, he chipped the date 1773 on the king beam, collected his dues, and went on to the next job.

It is interesting to note that the first occupant of the cottage when preparing for Christmas in that year would be unaware of the exciting events happening on the other side of the Atlantic, which would have such influence upon the lives of his children, and those who would follow them, as tenants of the farmer. The Boston Tea Party would mean nothing to him, as he brought in his Christmas logs for the hearth. But a hundred and seventy years later, Americans would live under that thatched roof, in time of war, and be welcomed by the villagers of Fairacre.

By that time, the modest two-up-and-two-down cottage had been enlarged so that there were three bedrooms and a bathroom upstairs, and a large kitchen below. The lean-to, of its earlier days, which had housed the wash tub, the strings of onions and the dried bunches of herbs for winter seasoning, had vanished. Despite war-time stringencies, the house was cared for and the garden trim, and the owner John Phipps, serving with his regiment, longed for the day of his return.

It never came. He was killed in the Normandy landings on D-Day, and the house was sold. It changed hands several times, and partly because of this, and partly because of its retired position, about a mile from the centre of Fairacre, Holly Lodge always seemed secret and aloof. The people who took it were always 'outsiders', retired worthies from Caxley in the main, with grown-up families and a desire for a quiet life in a house small enough to be manageable without domestic help.

The last couple to arrive, some two hundred years after the builder had carved his date on the king beam, were named Benson. Ambrose Benson was a retired bank manager from Caxley and his wife Joan, once a school mistress, was a bustling sixty-year-old. Their only son was up at Cambridge, their only daughter married with three children.

Fairacre, as always, was interested to see the preparations being made before the couple moved in. The holly hedge, unfortunately, screened much activity, and the fact that Holly Lodge was some distance from the village itself dampened the usual ardour of the gossip hunters. Nevertheless, it was soon learned that an annexe was being built at one end of the house, comprising a sitting-room, bedroom, bathroom and kitchen which would be occupied by Mrs Benson's elderly mother.

Mr Willet, caretaker of Fairacre School, sexton of St Patrick's and general handyman to the whole village, was the main source of such snippets of news about Holly Lodge as were available. The builder of the annexe, although a Caxley man, was a distant cousin of Mrs Willet's, and asked if her husband could give a hand laying a brick path round the new addition.

It was a job after Mr Willet's heart. He enjoyed handling the old rosy bricks, matching them for colour, aligning them squarely, and making a lasting object of beauty

and use. All his spare time, in the month before the Bensons were due to take over, he spent in their garden at his task, humming to himself as he worked.

His happiness was marred only by his impatience with the dilatory and slapdash ways of the builders.

'To see them sittin' on their haunches suppin' tea,' said Mr Willet to his friend Mr Lamb, the postmaster at Fairacre, 'fair makes my blood boil. And that fathead of a plumber has left the new bath standing in the middle of the lawn so that there's a great yellow mark where the grass has been killed.'

'Marvellous, ennit!' agreed Mr Lamb. 'D'you reckon they'll get in on time?'

'Not the way those chaps are carrying on,' snorted Mr Willet. 'Be lucky to get in by Christmas, if you ask me.'

Mr Willet's contribution to the amenities of Holly Lodge was finished before the end of August. The Bensons had hoped to be in residence by then but, as Mr Willet had forecast, they had to await the departure of the plasterer, the painters and the plumber.

At last, on a mercifully fine October day, the removal vans rolled up, and Fairacre had the pleasure of knowing that the newcomers had really arrived.

Joan Benson was soon studied, discussed and finally approved by the village. She was a plump, bird-like little woman, quick in speech and movement, given to wearing pastel colours and rather more jewellery than Fairacre was used to. Nevertheless, she was outstandingly friendly. She joined the Women's Institute and made a good impression by offering to help with the washing-up, a task which the local gentry tended to ignore.

Even Mrs Pringle, the village's arch-moaner, had to admit that 'she'd settled in quite nice for a town woman,' but could not resist adding that 'Time-Alone-Would-Tell'. Ambrose Benson was not much seen in the village, but it was observed that the garden at Holly Lodge was being put into good shape after the ravages of the builders' sojourn, and that he seemed to be enjoying his retirement in the new home.

Mr Partridge, the vicar of Fairacre, had called upon his new parishioners and had high hopes of persuading Ambrose Benson to take part in the numerous village activities which needed just such a person as a retired bank manager to see to them. How had Fairacre managed to muddle along before the arrival, Ambrose began to wonder, as he listened to the good vicar's account of the pressing needs of various committees, but naturally, he kept this thought to himself.

'A charming fellow,' Gerald Partridge told his wife. 'I'm sure he will be a great asset to Fairacre.'

The third member of the household was rarely seen. Joan's mother was eighty-seven, smitten with arthritis, and had difficulty in getting about. But the villagers agreed that she did the most beautiful knitting, despite her swollen fingers, and smiled very sweetly from the car when her daughter took her for a drive.

When the Bensons' first Christmas at Holly Lodge arrived, it was generally agreed in Fairacre that the vicar might be right.

Ambrose Benson, his wife and mother-in-law could well prove to be an asset to the village.

The winter was long and hard. It was not surprising that little was seen of the newcomers. Holly Lodge, snug behind the high hedge which gave it its name, seemed to be in a state of hibernation. Joan Benson was seen occasionally in the Post Office, or village shop, but Ambrose, it seemed, tended to have bronchial trouble and did not venture far in icy weather. As for old Mrs Penwood, her arthritis made it difficult to get from one room to the other, and she spent more and more time in the relative comfort of a warm bed.

'I shall be extra glad to see the Spring,' admitted Joan to Mr Lamb, as she posted a parcel to her daughter. 'My husband and mother are virtually housebound in this bitter weather. I long to get into the garden, and I know they do too.'

'Won't be long now,' comforted Mr Lamb, looking at the bleak village street through the window.

But Mr Lamb was wrong. Bob Willet, weather prophet among his many other roles, was stern in his predictions.

'We won't get no warmth till gone Easter,' he told those who asked his opinion. 'Then we'll be lucky. Might well be Whitsun afore it picks up.'

'Ain't you a Job's comforter, eh?' chaffed one listener. But he secretly respected Bob Willet's forecasts. Too often he was right.

On one of the darkest days of January, when a grey lowering sky gave the feeling of being in a tent, and Fairacre folk were glad to draw the blinds at four o'clock against such an inhospitable world, news went round the village grapevine that poor Ambrose Benson had been taken by ambulance to Caxley Hospital.

'Couldn't hardly draw breath,' announced Mrs Pringle, who had received the news via Minnie Pringle, her niece, who had had it from the milkman. 'Choking his life out, he was. I've always said that anything attacking the bronichals is proper cruel. It was congested bronichals that carried off my Uncle Albert, and him only fifty-two.'

The next day, the Bensons' daughter arrived, and the following day their son.

Gerald Partridge, the vicar, calling to offer sympathy and help, found the two ladies at Holly Lodge, red-eyed but calm.

'He is putting up a marvellous fight, they tell me,' said Joan Benson, 'and he has always been very fit, apart from this chest weakness. We are full of hope.'

'If there is anything I or my wife can do, please call

upon us,' begged the vicar. 'You are all very much in our thoughts, and we shall pray for your husband's recovery on Sunday morning.'

'You are so kind. We've been quite overwhelmed with sympathetic enquiries. Really, Fairacre is the friendliest place, particularly when trouble has struck.'

True to his word, Mr Partridge and his congregation prayed earnestly for Ambrose's restoration to health. But, even as they prayed, the sick man's life was ebbing, and by the time the good people emerged into St Patrick's wintry churchyard, Ambrose Benson had drawn his last painful breath.

This tragic blow, coming at the end of a long spell of anxiety, hit Joan cruelly. For years she and Ambrose had looked forward to his retirement. They had planned trips abroad, holidays in London where they could satisfy their love for the theatre, and, of course, the shared joys of the new home and its garden. Now all was shattered.

In a daze, she dealt with the dismal arrangements for the funeral, thankful to have her son and daughter with her over the first dreadful week of widowhood.

Luckily, Ambrose's affairs had been left in apple-pie order, as was to be expected from a methodical bank manager, but it was plain that Joan would need to be careful with money in the years ahead.

When her son and daughter departed, after the funeral, Joan was thankful to have the company of her mother in the house. The old lady seemed frailer than ever, and Joan took to sleeping in the spare bed put in her mother's room.

The annexe had been planned on one floor, and during

those nights when Joan lay awake, listening to the shallow breathing of her mother, and the queer little whimpers which she sometimes made unconsciously, as the arthritis troubled her dreams, she began to appreciate the charm of the new addition to Holly Lodge.

Sometimes she wondered if she might let it, and install her mother on the ground floor of the main house. Many a night was passed in planning rooms and arranging furniture, and this helped a little in mitigating the dreadful waves of grief which still engulfed her.

It was during this sad time that Joan found several true friends in Fairacre. Mrs Partridge and Mrs Mawne were particularly understanding, visiting frequently, and taking it in turns to sit with Mrs Penwood so that Joan could have a brief shopping expedition in Caxley, or a visit to old friends in the town.

She was met with sympathy and kindness wherever she went in the village, and became more and more determined to remain at Holly Lodge as, she felt sure, Ambrose would have wished her to do.

Spring was late in arriving, as Bob Willet had forecast, and it was late in April that the first really warm day came.

'I shall sit out,' said Mrs Penwood decidedly. 'Put my chair in the shelter of the porch, Joan, and I will enjoy the fresh air after all these months of being a prisoner.'

'It is still quite chilly,' said Joan. 'Do you think it is wise?'

'Of course it's wise!' responded her mother. 'It will do me more good than all the doctor's pills put together.'

With difficulty, Joan settled her mother in the sunshine. She was swathed in a warm cloak, and had a mohair rug

over her legs, but Joan was alarmed to find how cold her hands were when she took her some coffee.

Mrs Penwood brushed aside her daughter's protestations.

'I haven't been so happy since Ambrose—' she began, and hastily changed this to, 'for months. The air is wonderful. Just what I need.'

She insisted on having her light lunch outside, and Joan watched her struggling to hold a spoon with numbed fingers.

'Do come inside after lunch, mother,' she begged. 'You've really had the best of the day, you know.'

But the old lady was adamant. In some ways, thought Joan as she washed up, it was far simpler to cope with half a dozen children. At least they recognized authority, even if they did not always obey it. Old ladies, however sweet-natured, did not see why they should take orders from those younger than themselves.

She returned to find her mother sleeping, and decided to let her have another half an hour before she insisted on moving her indoors. Carefully, she spread another rug over the sleeping form, tucking the cold hands beneath it. Already the air was beginning to cool, and Joan went in to light the fire, ready for a cheerful tea-time.

A few minutes later, she heard cries and groans from her mother, and hurried outside. The old lady appeared to be having a spasm, and made incoherent noises. The only word which Joan could understand was the anguished cry of 'Pain, pain!'

Fear gave her strength to wrest the old lady, coverings and all, from the chair and to stumble with her to the bedroom in the annexe. Swiftly she managed to put her, still fully clothed, into bed, and ran to the telephone.

Their old family doctor from Caxley arrived within the hour, examined his patient minutely, and shook his head.

'I shall give her an injection now,' he told Joan. 'Just see that she remains warm and quiet. I will look in again after this evening's surgery.'

Joan nodded, too stricken to speak.

'Got a good neighbour handy to keep you company?' asked the doctor, knowing how recently she had been widowed.

'I will telephone the vicar's wife,' whispered Joan.

'I'll do it for you,' said the doctor.

Within five minutes, Mrs Partridge arrived, and the doctor went to his car.

'I'm afraid Mrs Penwood is in a pretty poor way,' he confided to the vicar's wife as she saw him off. 'It's a sad task to leave you with, but I will be back soon after seven.'

He was as good as his word. But when Mrs Partridge opened the door of Holly Lodge to him, he saw at once that his patient had gone.

Joan Benson spent that night, and the next one, at the vicarage, and the bonds formed then between the two women were to remain strong throughout their lives.

After this second blow, Joan went to stay for a time with her daughter. The children's chatter, and their need of her, gave her comfort, and she had time to try to put her plans in order.

She decided to stay. Holly Lodge might seem rather large for one widowed lady, but her children and grand-children would need bedrooms when they visited, and she did not want to part with much-loved possessions.

But the annexe, she decided, must be let. It was quite self-contained, and would make a charming home for some quiet woman in circumstances such as her own, or for that matter, for a mature woman with a job.

The Caxley Chronicle carried an advertisement in early June. Several people came to see Joan Benson but nobody seemed really suitable.

It was Henry Mawne, the vicar's friend and a dis-tinguished ornithologist, who first mentioned Miss Quinn.

'She's secretary to my old friend Barney Hatch in Caxley,' he told Joan. 'I know she needs somewhere. Her present digs are noisy, and she likes a quiet life. Nice woman, thirtyish, keeps old Barney straight, and that takes some doing. Like me to mention it?'

'Yes, please. I would be grateful.'

And thus it came about that Miriam Quinn, personal private secretary to Sir Barnabas Hatch, the financier, came to look at Holly Lodge's annexe one warm June evening, breathed in the mingled scent of roses and pinks, and surveyed the high hedge which ensured privacy, with the greatest satisfaction.

'I should like to come very much,' she said gravely to Joan Benson.

'And I,' said that lady joyfully, 'should like you to. Shall we go inside and settle things?'

CHAPTER TWO

Miss Quinn moved in on a still cloudless day in July. Fairacre was looking its best, as all downland country does, in summer heat.

Wild roses and honeysuckle embroidered the hedges. The cattle stood in the shade of the trees, swishing away the flies with their tails, and chewing the cud languorously. Dragonflies skimmed the surface of the diminishing river Cax, and a field of beans in flower wafted great waves of scent through the car's open window as Miss Quinn trundled happily towards her new home.

Before her the road shimmered waterily in the heat. It was almost a relief to enter the shady tunnel of trees at Beech Green, before regaining the open fields which led to Fairacre at the foot of the downs.

Her spirits rose as she left Caxley behind. Miriam Quinn had been brought up in a vicarage in a lonely stretch of the Fen country. Space and solitude were the two things which that windswept area had made essential to her happiness. Sometimes, when the canyons of some city streets drove her near to claustrophobic panic, she longed for the great Cambridge sky; and even the pleasant tree-lined road in Caxley, where she had lived since taking up the post with Sir Barnabas, she found stuffy and oppressive.

Now she would live in open country again. The encircling holly hedge, which gave her new abode its name, would not worry her. The windows of the annexe, she

had noticed swiftly, looked mainly upon the flank of the downs. She reckoned that she could see seven or eight miles to the distant woods to the south of Caxley from her sitting-room window.

She reached the signpost saying FAIRACRE 1, and began to look out for the hidden drive on her left which ran beside the high holly hedge to the main gate of Holly Lodge. It was propped open ready for her, she was grateful to see, and her own garage had its door hospitably open.

Miriam Quinn shut the car door and stood for a moment savouring the peace and the blessed coolness of the downland air. Bees hummed among the lime flowers above her, and a tabby cat rolled luxuriously in a fine clump of cat-mint in the sunny border.

Some distance away, Miriam discerned the figure of her new landlady. She was asleep in a deckchair, her head in the shade of a cherry tree, her feet propped up on a footstool in the sunshine.

Intense happiness flooded Miriam's being. The atmosphere of country tranquillity enveloped her like some comforting cloak in bitter weather. Here was home! Here was the peace she sought; the perfect antidote to the hectic atmosphere and pace of the office!

Very quietly, she picked up her case and made her way to the annexe door.

Joan Benson woke with a start and looked at her wrist watch. Almost four o'clock. Good heavens, she must have slept for nearly two hours! Since her mother's death she had found herself taking cat-naps like this, and friends told her that it was nature's way of restoring her after the stress of tending the invalids of the family for so long.

She became conscious of faint noises from the annexe. Of course, Miss Quinn would have arrived! How shameful not to be awake to greet her!

She struggled from the deck chair, and hastened towards

the house to make amends. Miriam Quinn received her apologies with a smile.

'I am going to make tea,' said her new landlady. 'Do join me in the garden. You know that I want you to look upon it as your own. Please feel free to use it whenever you like. I have put up a little washing line for you, behind the syringa bushes. But I will show you everything after tea.'

She was as good as her word. Tea had obviously been prepared with some care. There were homemade scones, and tomato sandwiches, and some delicious shortbread. Miss Quinn could see that Joan Benson was glad to have company, and was equally anxious to be hospitable. She chattered happily as she took her lodger round the garden, pointing out new improvements which Ambrose had made, and the herb patch which she herself had laid out.

'Take what you need,' she urged. 'There is plenty here for us both.'

'You are very kind, Mrs Benson.'

'Oh, do please call me "Joan",' she cried. 'We surely know each other well enough for Christian names.'

'Then you must call me "Miriam",' she responded.

'That's so much more friendly,' agreed her landlady, leading the way back to the house. 'You'll come in for a sherry later on, I hope.'

Miriam chose to treat this as a question rather than a statement.

'I think I ought to get on with my unpacking, if you don't mind,' she replied. 'And I have one or two telephone calls to make.'

'Of course, of course,' agreed Joan warmly. 'I think

you'll find the extension telephone convenient in your sitting-room. I very rarely use the one in my hall.'

She bustled off to collect the tea tray and Miriam returned to the peace of her own small domain. She sat looking at the distant view from the window, marshalling her thoughts.

She could be happy here, and Joan Benson was extremely kind and welcoming. Nevertheless, a small doubt disturbed her peace of mind.

Here they were, within one hour of her moving in, on Christian name terms, and her head already throbbing with the pleasant but interminable chatter of her hostess. She was experienced enough to realise that a recently bereaved woman must be lonely and more than usually grateful for company. The thing was – was she willing to give the time and sympathy which Joan so obviously needed at the moment?

She recognized her own limitations. She liked her own company. She liked the tranquillity of her natural surroundings. She had more than enough people around her during office hours, and Holly Lodge would be, she hoped, her refuge from them. It would be sad if her contented solitude were shattered by the well-meaning overtures of her landlady.

She stood up abruptly, and began to sort out her books. She was going too fast! Of course, Joan would be extra forthcoming at their first meeting. She would be anxious to put her lodger at ease. She must respond as well as her more reserved nature would permit. Joan deserved much sympathy, and was tackling her difficulties with considerable bravery, she told herself as she tried to come to terms with her new situation.

She lay in bed that night feeling the light breeze blowing across the miles of downland and cooling her cheeks. Somewhere a screech owl gave its eerie cry. A moth pattered up and down the window pane, and the fragrance from Joan's stocks scented the bedroom.

Miriam sighed happily. How quiet it was, after the noise of Caxley! What bliss to live here! She had not felt so free and relaxed since her far-off days in the Cambridgeshire vicarage.

It was all going to be perfect, she told herself sleepily. Quite perfect! Quite perfect – unless Joan became too—

She drifted into sleep.

She woke early and went to the window to savour the unbelievable freshness of the morning. Nothing stirred, except a pair of blackbirds busy among the rose bushes. A blue spiral of smoke rose in the distance. An early bonfire, she wondered? Or, more probably, the smoke from the chimney of a cottage hidden from view in a fold of the downs?

She bathed and dressed, relishing the privacy of her little house, and sat down to her toast and coffee soon after seven. There was no sound from next door, and she chided herself for feeling so relieved. Her need for solitude was even greater than usual first thing in the morning, and she sipped her coffee in contentment, looking around the kitchen and making a note of things yet to be done.

A rattling at the front door disturbed her train of thought. A letter lay on the mat, and as she picked it up she heard the postman pushing the mail through Joan's letter-box.

Her own missive was from Eileen, her sister-in-law, and consisted of two pages of good wishes for Miriam's future happiness in the new house, and news of the three children and Lovell, her husband and Miriam's only brother, two years her senior.

It was good of her to trouble to write, thought Miriam, but really, what an appalling hand she had, and why so many underlinings and exclamation marks? She poured out her second cup of coffee, and pondered on her sister-in-law's inability to buy envelopes which matched the writing paper, and to use a pen which wrote without dropping blots of ink. Such untidiness must irk Lovell as much as it did herself, for they were both neat and methodical, and had been so since childhood.

They had always been devoted to each other, and she remembered her grief when he had gone away to school. He had written regularly, in his neat small handwriting, so different from the untidy scrawl now before her.

From Cambridge he had followed his father into the Church, and was now vicar in a large parish, not far from Norwich, in the East Anglian countryside they both knew so well. Here he had met Eileen, soon after his arrival, and ever since then a certain bleakness had entered Miriam's life.

The old warm comradeship had gone, although no word was ever uttered. Miriam could understand her brother's love for the girl who so soon became his wife, but she could not help resenting her presence, try as she would.

Eileen was small and pretty, with an appealing air of fragility. Her fluffy fair hair was bound with ribbon. Her tiny shoes were bedecked with bows. She liked light historical novels, chocolate mints, deckle-edged writing paper and pale blue furnishings. She chattered incessantly and laughed a great deal. There was an air of teasing frivolity about her which would have earned her the title of 'minx' in earlier days. She was a complete contrast to the sober and dark-haired Miriam and Lovell, and their earnest parents. It was hardly surprising that Lovell was captivated. He had never met anyone quite so adorable.

On the whole, the marriage had turned out well, despite the Quinns' private misgivings. Eileen had produced three attractive children, the youngest now almost two years old, and although they were allowed far too much licence by their grandparents' standards, Miriam recognized that Eileen was a natural mother, quick to notice ailments and danger, although slap-dash in her methods of upbringing. Her innate playfulness made her a good companion to the young things, and if discipline was needed – and often it was, for they were high-spirited children – then Lovell reproved them with due solemnity.

Yes, things could have been much worse, Miriam told herself, stacking the breakfast things neatly. Lovell seemed happy enough, although one could not help wishing that he had found someone with a depth of character and outlook to match his own. But would she have liked such a woman any more than she liked Eileen?

She washed up thoughtfully, and was honest enough to admit that any woman whom Lovell married would have caused the same secret unhappiness. She had been supplanted, and it rankled. It was the outcome of unusual devotion between brother and sister, and she had now learned to live with this unpalatable fact.

She took a last look at herself in the long looking-glass

in her bedroom. Her thick dark hair was knotted on her neck. Her navy blue linen frock suited her slim build perfectly, and the plain but expensive shoes matched it exactly. She looked what she was – an attractive efficient business woman in her thirties.

'I wonder why she never married?' she had heard people say.

She wondered herself sometimes. There had been young men in her life, friends of Lovell's, for instance, when he was at Cambridge. Young and friendly, some of them ardent, they had been glad to visit the austere vicarage in the Fens, to enjoy the homely hospitality offered there and the company of Lovell's quiet younger sister.

But, cool and far-seeing, Miriam found none of them as attractive as the prospect of a life free of domestic responsibilities, free of children and free of a life-long partnership which she doubted if she could sustain. With her upbringing, marriage would be for life, and sometimes, watching her hard-working mother, she wondered if she would ever be as selfless.

Single life had its compensation. If she had to stay late at the office, or decided to go straight from there to see a play in London, or to visit friends, then there was no one to inform or to consider. Her decisions needed no discussion with another. Everything was under control.

No one stirred next door as she drove her car towards the gate. The road was empty. The horizon was as clear as her own mind. The day was mapped out. She knew exactly what would be happening at any given time. It was good to know where one was going.

Miriam Quinn was very sure of herself.

*

Within the next few weeks, news of the efficient paragon who lived in Mrs Benson's annexe had flashed round the village bush telegraph. Henry Mawne was largely to blame.

Gerald Partridge, the vicar, was in sore need of someone to look after the books of the Church Fabric Fund. Henry Mawne, honorary secretary and treasurer to a score or more village concerns, stated flatly that he could not take on any more.

'But what about that nice Miriam Quinn?' he asked of his friend. 'We met her the other night at Joan Benson's.'

'But she must be very busy with her job,' protested the vicar.

'She's home by about six. Why not ask her if she would like the job? She might be glad to meet people.'

The same kindly thought had occurred to other people in Fairacre, particularly those on committees needing secretaries, treasurers and the vague amorphous quality called 'new blood'. Here was a clever woman, obligingly free of family ties, in good health and possibly lonely, who could prove a godsend to the various organizations in need to help.

Henry Mawne was the first to approach Miriam on behalf of the short-staffed Church Fabric committee. She welcomed him to her shining home, gave him sherry, sparkled at his jokes, and declined the invitation in the most charming manner. Henry retired, hardly realizing that he had been defeated.

The Brownies needed a Brown Owl, the Cubs an Akela. The Women's Institute needed a book-keeper as the last one still worked in shillings and pence, and in any case had lost the account book. The Over Sixties' Club could do with a speaker on any subject, at any time suitable to Miss Quinn.

The Naturalists' Association, the Youth Club, the Play Group, the Welfare Clinic, St Patrick's Choir and the Sunday School were anxious to have Miss Quinn's presence and support, and Miriam soon realized, with amusement and resignation, that much more hummed beneath Fairacre's serene face than she had imagined.

Her tact, her charm and her intelligence, backed by her formidable resolve to keep her life exactly as she wanted it, enabled her to stay clear of any of these entanglements.

Baffled, and slightly hurt, the villagers retired worsted.

Mrs Pringle summed up the general feeling about the newcomer.

'No flies on Miss Quinn! She knows her value, that one, but she ain't for sale!'

CHAPTER THREE

As the weeks passed, Miriam's pleasure grew. Holly Lodge was all that she had hoped for – peaceful, convenient and set among the great windswept countryside for which she had craved.

She took to strolling for an hour each evening before her supper. The air blew away the little tensions and annoyances of the office, and she always returned refreshed.

Sometimes she explored the village of Fairacre, stopping to talk politely to all who accosted her, but as Mr Lamb at the Post Office said: 'She don't make the running. It's you who has to start the conversation, though she's as nice as pie once you get going.'

Henry Mawne and his wife she knew through her employer, and had been invited to their Queen Anne house at the end of the village, on several occasions. The Hales at Tyler's Row, the Partridges at the vicarage, Mr Willet and Mrs Pringle, all were known to her, and she was on nodding terms with the majority of Fairacre's inhabitants.

But, on the whole, she preferred to ramble in the immediate vicinity of Holly Lodge. There she was unlikely to meet well-meaning folk who engaged her in conversation. She revelled in these solitary walks, noting the nuts and berries in the hedges, the flight of the downland birds, and the small fragrant flowers which flourished on the chalky soil.

She skirted the field of barley behind the house when she set off for the downs. Since her coming, the crop had turned from green to gold, fine and upstanding, with heavy ears. She watched it being harvested in August, and listened to the regular thumping of the baler as she ate her simple evening meal in the sitting-room or carried her tray to some quiet corner of the garden.

Joan Benson had quickly realized that the girl preferred to be alone, and she sympathized with her feelings. After all, she told herself, Miriam arrived home tired, having dealt with people and their problems all day.

She had met Sir Barnabas Hatch at the Mawnes and had summed him up astutely as the sort of man who, endowed with twice the average amount of energy and intelligence, expects other people to be equally dynamic. Miriam could well hold her own, and her cool disposition would enable her to cope with any outbursts from her employer. Nevertheless, he must be a demanding person with whom to deal and it was no wonder that the girl needed the peace of her little home at the end of the day.

But although she respected Miriam's desire for privacy, she could not help feeling a little disappointed. She had hoped for company, and although the mere presence of someone next door was a great comfort, she sorely missed the conversation and company of her husband and mother. She found herself switching on the radio, simply to hear another voice during the day, or making some excuse to walk to the village to enjoy a few words with anyone she met.

The days grew shorter. Joan tidied her garden, strung up her onions, planted bulbs and had a massive autumn bonfire which wreathed blue smoke around Holly Lodge for two whole days. She was stirring the last of its embers one Saturday afternoon when Miriam waved to her from the other end of the garden.

'I'm off blackberrying,' she called. 'Shall I pick some for you?'

Joan dropped the hoe she had been using as an outsize poker, and hurried across.

'I'll join you, if I may,' she said. 'I've been meaning to go all the week. Wait half a minute while I fetch a basket.'

Miriam rather welcomed company on this golden afternoon. She had finished the usual weekend chores of washing and shopping. The tradesmen had been paid their weekly dues, the house was clean. The mending awaited her, but otherwise her affairs were in as much apple-pie order here as they were at the office. It would be good to hear Joan's news. She felt slightly guilty about seeing so little of her lately. This afternoon she would make amends.

The two women strode across the stubble of the field to a tall hedge. The sharp straw caught their legs, but it was wonderfully exhilarating to feel the crunch of it beneath their feet. At the farther edge of the field Miriam caught sight of something moving.

'Look!' she said, grasping Joan's arm. 'A covey of partridges! There must be at least ten young ones running along there. I haven't seen that for a long time.'

Joan was struck, for the first time, with the excitement in her companion's face.

'You really are a country girl!' she exclaimed. 'Somehow I hadn't realized it.'

Miriam smiled at her.

'It's why I love Holly Lodge so much,' she told her.

The blackberries were thick and the two women picked steadily. Jet-black, ruby-eyed and pale green, the berries cascaded down the hedge. United in their task, relaxed by the sunshine and sweet air, they talked of this and that, Miriam more forthcoming than ever before, and Joan relishing the chance to chatter again.

An onlooker might have learnt a great deal about the two women's natures, simply by watching their methods of picking. Miriam chose her bush with a shrewd eye to size and ripeness, and then picked swiftly and systematically, from the fat terminal berry, along the sides of the branch until all were gathered. Her movements were rapid but controlled, and not one berry was dropped.

Joan ambled happily between bushes, picking only the large ones. She lacked the concentration of the younger woman, but obviously enjoyed her haphazard forays and was quite content to have only half a basket of fruit, compared with Miriam's brimming one, when the time came to return home.

'I'm going to make tea,' said Miriam. 'Come and join me.'

Joan was delighted to accept, and after depositing her basket in her own kitchen and washing her battle-scarred hands, she returned to the annexe bearing some bronze chrysanthemums.

'I love them,' said Joan, watching her neighbour arrange them, 'but I always feel rather sad. They mean the summer's over. Still, they are very beautiful, and have such a marvellous scent. Rather like very expensive furniture polish, I always think.'

Miriam let her chatter happily, wondering how to broach a subject which had been in her mind for some time.

'Would you mind if I redecorated these rooms, Joan?'

'Not at all,' she said, looking a little surprised. 'But they were done, you know, very recently.'

'That's why I haven't liked to mention it. But, to tell you the truth, I'm not a lover of cream walls, and with this old mahogany I thought a very pale green would look well.'

Joan nodded approvingly.

'It would indeed. Would you get somebody in to do it? I'm sure Mr Willet could recommend someone reliable. Shall I ask him?'

'No, there's no need. I shall enjoy tackling it myself. I'm quite experienced.'

'What a lot of talents you have! When would you want to start? Can I help at all?'

Miriam began to feel the familiar qualms of apprehension returning.

'I may take a few days off,' she said guardedly. 'I have some time owing to me, and Barnabas has to make a trip overseas soon. I may be able to arrange something then. If not, I could probably do some of it at Christmas time.'

This chance remark sent Joan along a new path.

'I'm writing to my two children this week to see if they can join me for Christmas. I thought if they had plenty of notice, I should have more chance of their company. It would be lovely to have the house full and you could meet them all. Barbara's babies are such fun.'

Miriam's heart sank.

'You're very kind,' she murmured. 'More tea?'

'I simply adore Christmas,' continued Joan, stirring her second cup. 'And Fairacre is the perfect place to spend it. Lots of little parties, and carol singers coming to the door and having a drink and mince pies when they've finished; and always such lovely services at St Patrick's with the church decked beautifully with holly and ivy. Christmas really is *Christmas* at Fairacre!'

Miriam's polite smile masked her inner misgivings. Christmas at the vicarage had always meant a particularly busy day for her father, and a considerable number of elderly relatives who had been invited by her kindly mother because as she said: 'They had nowhere else to go, poor things, and one can't think of them alone at Christmas.'

Miriam had long ago given up feeling guilty about her dislike of Christmas festivities, and latterly had taken pains to keep her own Christmases as quiet as possible. This year she was determined to spend it alone in her new abode, with no turkey, no pudding, no mince pies and – definitely – no holly.

She might have a glass of the excellent port which Barnabas usually gave her with her customary light lunch, and she intended to read some Trollope, ear-marked for the winter months. But too much food, too much noise and, above all, too much convivial company she would avoid.

But would she be able to?

She looked at dear kind Joan, rosy with fresh air and relaxed with warmth and company. How she blossomed, thought Miriam, with other people about!

No wonder she loved Christmas. Visiting, and being visited, was the breath of life to the good soul, and the joy of the festival would far outweigh any extra work which it entailed.

'I must be off,' said Joan, struggling to her feet. 'There's bramble jelly to be made next door and I must leave you to tackle your own.'

Miriam closed the door behind her, and returned to the sitting-room deep in thought. It looked as though evading action might well be needed as Christmas approached.

She looked out upon the golden evening. The trees were beginning to turn tawny with the first cool winds of autumn.

Ah well, she told herself, time enough yet to postpone such troubles!

But the autumn slipped by at incredible speed. It was dark now when Miriam left the office. She was glad to nose her car into the garage and hurry into the annexe to light the fire, which she prudently set in readiness in the morning.

The force of the equinoctial gales surprised her. Now she began to realize how open to the elements was this high downland country, and to appreciate the sagacity of the past owner of Holly Lodge who had had the foresight to plant the thick hedge which gave the house not only its name, but considerable protection from the blasts of winter.

Her own little home gave her increasing satisfaction. She had painted the kitchen white. It took three weekends of hard work to do the job, but Miriam was a perfectionists, and she rubbed down the old paint until not one scrap remained, before she began to apply the undercoat with a steady hand. She enjoyed the work, she exulted in the finished result and, above all, she relished the perfect quiet as she got on with the job.

She was even more determined now to tackle the sitting-room at Christmas. Barney, as she thought of him, was making a business trip to Boston and New York, leaving on December 16 and not returning until after New Year's Day. Miriam had already made the flight bookings for him and for Adèle, his wife. They were meeting their only daughter, who was married to an American, and proposed to spend Christmas at her home and to see their grandchildren. Miriam had been requested to find some toys suitable for children aged six and eight.

'The sort of thing they won't get over there, you know,' said Barney vaguely. 'Adèle's got the main things, but I'd like to take something myself. I'll leave it to you. Not too weighty, of course, because of flying.'

'I won't get an old English rocking-horse,' promised Miriam.

'Oh no! Nothing like that!' exclaimed Sir Barnabas, looking alarmed. Humour, even as obvious as this, did not touch him. 'And no more than five pounds apiece,' he added. He was not a businessman for nothing.

Miriam promised to do her best.

As Christmas approached, the whirl of village activities quickened. Posters went up on barn doors, on the trunks of trees, and on the bus shelter near the church, drawing attention to the usual Mammoth Jumble Sale, the Fur and Feather Whist Drive and the Social and Dance, all to be held – on different dates, of course – under the roof of the Village Hall.

As well as these advertised delights, there were more private junketings, such as the Women's Institute Christmas party, Fairacre School's concert and a wine and cheese party for the Over-Sixties' Club.

An innovation was Mrs Partridge's Open Day at the vicarage, which was her own idea, and to which the village gave considerable attention.

'You can just pop in there,' said Mrs Willet, in the Post Office, 'any time between ten o'clock and seven at night. You pays ten pence to go in, and you pays for your cup of coffee, or your dinner midday, or tea, say, at four o'clock.'

'And what, pray,' said Mrs Pringle, who was buying stamps, 'do you get for dinner? And how much will it be?'

'I think it's just soup and bread and cheese,' said Mrs Willet timidly.

Mrs Pringle snorted, and two stamps fluttered to the ground.

'I don't call that DINNER,' boomed the lady, preparing to bend to retrieve the stamps.

'Here, let me,' said Mr Lamb, the postmaster, hurrying to rescue Mrs Pringle's property. More than likely to have a heart attack, trying to bend over in those corsets, was his ungallant private comment, as he proffered the stamps with a smile.

'Ta,' said Mrs Pringle perfunctorily. She turned again upon little Mrs Willet.

'And *how much* for this 'ere rubbishy snack?'

'I'm not sure,' faltered Mrs Willet. 'It's for charity, you see. Half to the Church Fabric Fund and half to some mission in London that the vicar takes an interest in. Poor people, you know.'

'*Poor people?*' thundered Mrs Pringle. 'In London? Why, we've got plenty of poor in Fairacre as could do with a bit of help at Christmas, without giving it away to foreigners up London. Look at them Coggses! They could do with a bit of extra. That youngest looks half-starved to me.'

'Well, whose fault's that?' asked Mr Lamb, entering the fray. 'We all know Arthur drinks his pay packet – always has done, and always will. If he was given more, he'd drink that too.'

'Who said give Arthur the money?' demanded Mrs Pringle, her four chins wobbling with indignation. 'Give it to that poor wife of his, I say, to get a decent meal for the kids.'

'They do get something from the Great Coal Charity,' said Mrs Willet diffidently.

Mrs Pringle brushed this aside. 'And in my mother's time there wasn't no Great Coal Charity to rely on,' she boomed on.

'She didn't have anything from the Great Coal Charity,' responded Mr Lamb, 'because there wasn't one then.'

'I'll have you know,' said Mrs Pringle with devastating dignity, 'that that there Charity was started in seventeen fifty because the vicar told us himself at a talk he gave the W.I.'

'Maybe,' replied Mr Lamb, 'but it was started as a *Greatcoat* Charity, and six deserving old men and six deserving old women got a woollen greatcoat apiece to keep out the winter cold.'

Mrs Pringle looked disbelieving, her mouth down-turned like a disgruntled turtle's.

'And what happened,' said Mr Lamb, warming to his theme, 'was this. Someone left the crossing off the "t" in "coat" when they was writing up the minutes about

37

George the Fourth's time, and so it went on being called the Great Coal Charity, and instead of a coat you get coal.'

'Well, I never,' exclaimed Mrs Willet. 'I never heard that before!'

'Nor did I,' said Mrs Pringle, with heavy sarcasm. She picked up her stamps and made for the door.

'Which doesn't alter my feelings about bread and cheese dinners. What's dinner without a bit of meat on your plate?'

She banged the door behind her. Mrs Willet sighed.

'That woman,' said Mr Lamb, 'makes me come over prostrate with dismal when she shows that face of hers in here. Now, love, what was it you wanted?'

CHAPTER FOUR

Miriam was wise enough to realize that she could not opt out of Christmas activities completely. Nor did she wish to. She willingly provided boxes of chocolates for raffle prizes at various Fairacre functions, accompanied Joan to a carol service at St Patrick's and drank a glass of sherry at the vicarage Open Day.

There was no doubt about it, this new venture was extremely popular with Fairacre folk. Mrs Partridge and her helpers had decked the downstairs rooms with scarlet and silver ribbons, and all the traditional trappings of Christmas. Holly and ivy, mistletoe and glittering baubles added their beauty, and an enormous Christmas tree dominated the entrance hall.

In each room was a table bearing goods suitable for Christmas presents, and a brisk trade ensured that the Church Fabric Fund and Mr Partridge's pet mission would profit. Miriam recognized the planning which must have gone into this enterprise, and admired the efficiency with which it was run. It was an idea she intended to pass on to Lovell, when she saw him, for future use in his own parish.

These little jaunts she thoroughly enjoyed, and she was grateful for the genuine welcome she was given by her village neighbours. Joan's growing excitement, as the festival approached, was a source of mingled pleasure and apprehension, however.

'Isn't it wonderful?' Joan had said, on the morning of

the Open Day. 'Roger is coming for Christmas, after all, and then going with a party of other young people to Switzerland for the winter sports.'

'Marvellous,' agreed Miriam. Barbara, the daughter, her husband and three children had already accepted Joan's invitation and would be in the house for a week. Miriam had listened patiently to Joan's ecstatic arrangements of sleeping, feeding and entertaining the family party for the last week or two. The plans were remarkably fluid, and Miriam had long since given up trying to keep track of who slept where, or when would be best to eat the turkey.

It was quite apparent that she must meet Joan's family at some time, and she had accepted an invitation to have a drink on Christmas Eve. So far she had managed to evade the pressing invitations to every meal which her kind-hearted landlady issued daily. That sitting-room would be painted, come hell or high water, she told herself grimly!

She had arranged with Barney to take some time off during his absence in America. This would give her a few days before Christmas to get on with her decorating, having left the office in apple-pie order after his departure. Tins of paint and three new brushes waited on the top shelf in the kitchen, and she felt a little surge of happiness every time she saw them. She could see the sitting-room, in her mind's eye, a bower of green and white, all ready for the New Year, and the new curtains and cushions she had promised herself.

Almost all her Christmas presents were wrapped and ready to post. Christmas cards began to arrive thick and fast. Usually, she had some plan of display – a white-washed branch to hold them, or scarlet ribbons placed across the walls. But this year she read each with interest and then slipped it into a folder brought from the office, so that all were stacked away, leaving the sitting-room ready for her ministrations.

She was glad when the time came to leave the office for her extended Christmas break. Four days after Barney's departure, with everything left tidy, she distributed her presents to the office staff, and thankfully set off for Fairacre and the decorating.

Lights were strung across the streets of Caxley, and entwined the lamp standards. Christmas trees jostled pyramids of oranges in the greengrocers' shops. Turkeys hung in rows in the butchers', presenting their pink plump breasts for inspection. Children flattened their noses against the windows of the toy shops, while exhausted mothers struggled with laden shopping baskets and wondered what they had forgotten.

Queues formed at the Post Offices, buying stamps for stacks of Christmas cards, weighing parcels bedizened with Christmas stickers, or simply enquiring, with some agitation, the last date for posting to New Zealand and getting the answer they had feared. Yet again, Aunt Flo in Wellington would receive a New Year's card sent by air mail.

The surging crowds, the garish lights, the sheer unappetizing commercialism of the festival disgusted Miriam as she threaded her way slowly along the busy streets. It was good to gain the country road to Fairacre, climbing steadily towards the downs, to smell the frosty air and to know that peace lay ahead, behind the holly hedge.

She spent most of the evening by the fire, relishing her solitude and making plans for the attack on the painting. She reviewed the situation and found it highly satisfactory. Her posting was done. A box containing Christmas presents, to be given by hand to Joan and other local friends, was on a shelf in the kitchen cupboard. The milkman was going to deliver a small chicken in two days' time, ready for her modest Christmas dinner. Christmas boxes for the tradesmen waited on the hall window-sill for distribution as they called.

Nothing – but *nothing* – she told herself with satisfaction, could keep her from her decorating now!

Fired by the thought, she began to gather together the ornaments about the room, stacking them in a large cardboard box. It would save time in the morning, when she would roll up the carpet, take down the curtains and push the large pieces of furniture into the centre of the room. Already she had found two dust sheets to cover the mound, and had planned the best method of building the assorted shapes of sofa, chairs and table into a compact pile. Her methodical mind revelled in such practical arrangements. The job was going to be as efficiently tackled as any at the office, and would give her far more satisfaction.

She prepared the room next morning, and by midday was down to the exacting job of washing down the old paint, and rubbing down any uneven patches on the surface. Joan came in once or twice to see if there was anything she could do to help. Miriam greeted her with a smile, but was obviously so content to work alone that Joan retired after expressing admiration for Miriam's zeal.

'It's going to look marvellous,' she cried. 'Will you have lunch with me? It will save you cooking.'

'I've made a sandwich,' replied Miriam, 'and shall have it with some coffee to save time, if you don't mind.'

Joan was secretly rather relieved. Her whole attention now was on the arrival of Barbara and family in two days time. After the loneliness of the past months, it was pure joy for her to be preparing food, and decking the house, in readiness for the company which would bring Holly Lodge to life again.

Christmas Day fell on a Thursday. Miriam had high hopes of finishing the painting by then, although she faced the fact that the windows – always a tricky and tedious job – might have to be left for later. As Barney would not be back from America until January 3rd, she had planned to take another few days after Christmas if all were well at the office. There should be ample time to get the sitting-room into perfect order.

By Monday evening the first coat of emulsion paint was on the wall. She stood back, brush in hand, to admire its delicate shade. Yes, it was perfect!

Tomorrow she would put on the second and final coat, she told herself happily, going to the sink to rinse the paint brush. She could hear Joan talking to someone on the telephone. No doubt Barbara was ringing about the travelling plans.

But a moment later, Joan called to her. 'Your brother, Miriam, from Norfolk.'

'Right!' called the girl, drying her hands.

Lovell sounded agitated.

'I've trouble here,' said the deep voice. 'Eileen's just gone to hospital.'

'An accident?'

'No, nothing like that. But most acute stomach pains. Awful sickness. Probably something to do with the gall bladder. She's had this sort of thing off and on for some time, but this morning she had this really terrible attack.'

'Poor Eileen! Where is she? Far away?'

'No. In the local hospital. The thing is, can you possibly come and hold the fort for the next few days? I know it's asking a lot, but over Christmas I shall be extra busy in the parish, and I don't know which way to look for help with the children.'

'I can come,' said Miriam promptly. It was good to know that Lovell turned at once to her when he needed help. The old strong bond between them was re-established in those few words uttered so many miles apart.

'You're a trump, Miriam,' cried Lovell. The relief in his voice warmed her heart. 'I can't tell you how glad I am. And so will the children be, and Eileen, when I tell them.'

'I'll set off first thing,' said Miriam, 'and be with you tomorrow afternoon. Have you got provisions in, or shall I bring something?'

'Oh, I expect everything's here,' said Lovell, but he sounded somewhat vague.

There was a sound of an infant screaming in the background.

'Don't worry,' called Miriam hastily. 'I'll see to things when I arrive.'

'Marvellous!' sighed her brother.

The screaming became louder. Miss Quinn replaced the receiver and went sadly back to the half-painted sitting-room.

'Well,' she said glumly. 'That's that!'

Joan heard the news with distress. Anything to do with illness touched her sympathetic heart, and re-awakened memories of her own two recent bereavements. On this occasion there were further causes for dismay.

'And at Christmas too! And with children in the home! Dear, oh dear, it couldn't be more unfortunate, especially with the extra services your brother will have to take. If only I could help!'

'I know you would if you could, but you will have enough to do at Holly Lodge. I will telephone as soon as I get there tomorrow.'

There was nothing more to do to the painting until the

first coat was thoroughly dry. It should certainly be just that by the time she returned, she thought grimly. Understandable irritation began to flood her as she packed away the brushes and tins. How like Eileen to manage to mess up so many people's affairs!

Immediately she chided herself, but the resentment remained to rankle as she found her case and began to pack. And yet, in a distorted way, she almost felt grateful to Lovell's wife for giving her the chance to have his company for a few days of uninterrupted pleasure. It was years since they had been able to talk without the presence of her flibbertigibbet sister-in-law.

It took her longer to pack than usual. Clearing the sitting-room had meant stacking things in unaccustomed places, and she was hard put to it to find a map showing the route. At last, it turned up, packed among cookery books. Yes, skirt Oxford, make for Bicester, Buckingham, Bedford, Cambridge, Newmarket and then on into Norfolk. It was going to be a longish trip. She must start at first light, and pray for a fine day. There was no knowing what she would find to do when she arrived, and she only hoped that the bitter winter weather, for which East Anglia was noted, would hold off and enable her to return in good time. Oh, that poor sitting-room, she grieved!

She climbed into bed, turned out the light, and determined to put aside tomorrow's worries and get to sleep. The vision of a raddled old housemaid called, unbelievably, Euphrosyne, who had helped at her parents' vicarage, came into her mind.

'What can't be cured must be endured,' was one of her favourite sayings.

Maybe Euphrosyne had the last word there, thought Miriam, settling to sleep.

There was frost on the grass when Miriam looked out first thing in the morning. It was grey and still, overcast, but bitterly cold. In the fold of the downs, scarves of mist floated. No breeze stirred the bare branches, and the birds sat huddled in silence, awaiting any largesse thrown from the kitchen window.

It was a dispiriting sort of day, thought Miss Quinn, brewing her coffee. She only hoped that the mists of Fairacre were not an indication of fog in the flat fields of Bedfordshire and the Fen lands beyond.

She remembered the chill of Lovell's draughty vicarage, and went to look out two extra thick sweaters to throw into the back of the car with her wellington boots. Brought up in that bleak area of England, she prudently went prepared for the worst that the weather could do in December.

Joan called in soon after nine, bearing fruit, biscuits and a flask of coffee.

'I hope I'm in time. Have you made some sandwiches?'

'Well, no,' admitted Miriam, after thanking her. 'I thought I would stop on the way and have a proper lunch. I shall be ready for it, no doubt, and heaven alone knows if there will be anything prepared at Lovell's. I'm taking eggs for us all to be on the safe side.'

'Good. Do ring as soon as you arrive. I shall be anxious.'

'I will. And do use my bedroom while the family is here if it's any help. I have stripped the bed.'

Joan's face lit up.

'That would be marvellous, if you're sure. Roger could go there, or I could perhaps. How nice of you! I will work it out while I'm making the mince pies this morning.'

It was plain that this new turn would add agreeably to her multifarious plans, and Miriam was glad to see her so occupied.

By half past nine she was on her way, having said farewell to Joan and left her Christmas presents. The hedges were hoary with rime, and in each dip of the downs the mist still swirled. Thin ice crackled beneath the car wheels, and the whole world looked cold and unwelcoming. She thought with longing of the snug cottage she had left behind, and the work half done.

But duty, duty must be done,
The rule applies to everyone,
And painful though that duty be
To shirk the task were fiddle-de-dee

she sang aloud, cheering herself with the thumping rhythm, as the car sped onward.

To her relief, a watery sun, pallid as the moon, became visible through the clouds as she rattled along the road which by-passed Oxford. On each side lay water meadows, and the leaden sheen of the winding river, its course marked by willows stark in their winter nakedness.

As the sun's strength increased, so did Miss Quinn's spirits rise. It was good to see something different. Good to be visiting Lovell, even in such worrying circumstances. Good, even, to feel unaccustomed sympathy for the tiresome Eileen who had precipitated this journey. Looking after the three children Miriam viewed with some trepidation. They were healthy, high-spirited youngsters, and would no doubt be missing their mother. Miriam knew her limitations. She might be Barney's right hand. She might be the dragon that frightened the typing pool. Whether she would be as efficient as aunt-cum-housekeeper remained to be seen.

Bicester and Buckingham were passed. Strange, alien Wolverton, an industrial surprise among the flat fields, lay behind her. After Newport Pagnell, she told herself, she would find a likely-looking lane to enjoy Joan's coffee and fruit. Hunger began to assail her, but the sun now shone warmly, and the Midlands, which Hilaire Belloc had found 'sodden and unkind', lay ahead bathed in gentle light.

She turned into a by-lane where the hedge maple gleamed like gold. A robin flew on to a nearby twig, watching her closely. Crumbs had been known to come from car windows.

Miriam crushed one of Joan's biscuits and scattered it for her companion, who darted down to enjoy this unexpected feast.

Watching his sharp beak at work, Miriam sipped her steaming coffee. In amicable silence, the two strangers enjoyed their meal together.

CHAPTER FIVE

She broke her journey at Cambridge, partly because the place was full of happy memories of her own and Lovell's youth and, more practically, because she knew exactly where to go shopping.

She was lucky to find a parking space outside Queen's. Here, at a May Week ball long ago, she had met Martin Farrar, a friend of Lovell's, and had enjoyed a few weeks' mild flirtation with the handsome boy. Where was he now, she wondered? Farming somewhere in a nearby county, she seemed to remember Lovell saying one day – and happily married.

It was bitingly cold, despite the sunshine. The slow-moving Cam was dappled with the last yellow leaves of autumn, and a vicious little wind stirred the dust along Silver Street.

She bought fruit, bacon and sausages, enough to provide a supper and a breakfast to give her time to check the provisions in Eileen's store cupboard.

She also bought a bottle of sherry for Lovell and flowers for the invalid; and, at the last minute, dived into a shabby toy shop for crayons and balloons. Thus armed she returned to the car, and having deposited her purchases, decided to treat herself to a splendid lunch at the Garden House Hotel nearby.

She was on her way again, much fortified, within the hour.

As always, the miles seemed longer than ever after

Newmarket, as the wide heathlands stretched away into the distance, and the well-known East Anglian wind scoured the countryside.

It was almost dark by the time she arrived at the vicarage.

No one answered the bell which she pressed hopefully at the front door, so she pushed it open, to be greeted by the pungent smell of burning.

The wide hall ran from front door to a glass one at the back. Through it Miriam could see the shabby overgrown garden backed by a lowering sky.

Light spilled from a side door into the hall, and she

could hear children laughing. Obviously, all activity was centred in the kitchen.

'Anyone home?' she called advancing, her heels clicking on the black and white marble tiles. Not even a rush mat, thought Miss Quinn, to mitigate the piercing cold to one's feet!

There were screams of excitement as two little girls tumbled through the door, and rushed upon her.

'Auntie Miriam! You've come! We thought you'd be here when we'd gone to bed!'

Two pairs of sticky hands caressed her new Welsh tweed suit lovingly. She bent to kiss the children. The extraordinary smell seemed to envelop them.

'We're making toffee,' said Hazel importantly.

'Only it's a bit caught,' added Jenny. 'Come and see.'

She followed them into the kitchen. Hazel, the nine-year-old, led her to the electric stove. Jenny, two years younger, indicated the saucepan, and Miriam's heart plummeted.

A tar-like substance coated one of the open element electric plates, and made rivulets down the once white front of the stove.

The residue gleamed malevolently from the bottom of the buckled saucepan. That was one utensil, thought Miriam, which would have to be replaced.

'Where is the toffee?' she enquired.

'It's here, you see, but we just ran out into the garden to tell Daddy the telephone was ringing, and it all went sort of fizzy and buzzled all over the stove.'

'That's right,' corroborated Jenny, licking a sticky finger. 'It tastes funny, but it's set, hasn't it?'

'It certainly has,' said Miriam with distaste. 'Put it in the sink to soak.'

'But it's *toffee*,' wailed Jenny, sensing adult disapproval. 'We can *eat* it! There's a pound of sugar in it.'

'There's a pound of sugar,' agreed Miriam, 'but it's mostly over the stove. Cheer up, I'll make you some fudge instead. But where's Daddy?'

'He went to find Robin. He's in the garden somewhere. We'll show you.'

She followed their prancing fingers into the dusky garden. Both children were dark-haired, like their father, but she could not believe that she and Lovell had ever been quite so thin.

Did Eileen feed them properly, or were they allowed to leave food if they were too impatient to eat it? Time would tell.

In any case, they were not lacking in energy. They hopped and skipped ahead of her, leaping over brambles and tussocks of grass that must once have been a lawn in more spacious days.

'She's come! Daddy, she's come!' screamed the little girls, and out from behind a hedge came Lovell holding his youngest in his arms.

'You dear girl!' he cried, depositing Robin at his feet. He put his arms round Miriam in a bear hug. They had never been demonstrative, and this welcoming embrace made all the irritations of the journey drop away. His face was cold, his hair rough, and smelling of all outdoors: a wintry, bruised-grass, autumn-bonfire smell, as different from the acrid scent of burning which had greeted her as sea-mist is from Midland fog.

In that instant, she was transported back to their shared childhood when together they climbed trees, or

rolled, screaming with delight, down a grassy slope in the vicarage garden. Sudden tears pricked her eyes, and Lovell, holding her now at arm's length, said, 'You look cold. Come inside.'

The two little girls bounced ahead, but Robin held up his arms to be carried. Miriam watched Lovell hoist him aloft again, and thought how like his mother the young boy looked. He had the same fair hair and blue eyes, the wide brow and pointed chin which gave Eileen her child-like air.

She held out a hand to him, but he turned away from her, burying his face in his father's neck.

'That's no way to welcome an aunt,' chided Lovell. 'Why, she's going to be the angel in the house, if only you knew it!'

'Wait and see!' laughed Miriam, following her brother indoors.

It seemed to Miriam, as she surveyed the sitting-room where most of the family activities went on, that a strong charwoman, rather than an angel, was needed in the place.

Toys littered the table, the chairs and the carpet. Copper, the ageing cocker spaniel, was curled up on the rumpled cover of the couch in front of the fire. A log had rolled off, and lay mouldering in the hearth, filling the room with pungent smoke. A glass vase, containing six dead chrysanthemums and an inch of dark green slime, decorated the mantelpiece, with a half-eaten banana beside it.

Lovell, dropping Robin beside the spaniel, caught sight of his sister's face, and laughed.

'Ghastly, isn't it? We had a sort of scratch lunch, and that banana is Robin's contribution.'

'Well,' said Miriam, trying to sound briskly cheerful, 'that can soon be put right. What's happened to Annie?'

Annie was a young girl from the village who came for a couple of hours or so in the late afternoon each day to help Eileen with the children's tea and bathtime.

'She's off over Christmas,' explained Lovell. 'The family has gone to Ely to stay with the grandmother, but she will be back on Monday, I hope.'

Miriam hoped so too. She bent to remove a grubby handkerchief from Robin's grasp. He was busy wiping Copper's nose, and the dog resented it. The child set up an ear-splitting wail, and the two little girls rushed to comfort him.

Miriam hastily returned the handkerchief, and the wailing ceased as though a siren had been switched off.

'Perhaps I'd better take up my case,' she said to Lovell, 'and then I will cook a meal for us all.'

'Goody-goody!' shouted Hazel.

'Gum-drops!' yelled Jenny. 'That's what we say: "Goody-goody-gum-drops!" Do you say that? Do you say: "Goody-goody-gum-drops!" when you're pleased? We do, don't we, Hazel? We *always* say: "Goody-goody—"'

'Not now you don't,' said Lovell firmly. 'Let Aunt Miriam have a few minutes' peace. Shall I take you up?'

'No, no,' replied Miriam hastily. 'I expect I'm in the usual room, aren't I?'

'I'll come with you,' said Jenny.

'No, let me!' said Hazel.

'*Only one!*' bellowed Lovell, above the din. 'You show Aunt Miriam to her room, Hazel, and then come down again. We'll set the table in the kitchen.'

Miriam deposited her basket of groceries on the kitchen dresser, averting her eyes from the appalling state of the cooker. Hazel was swinging on the newel post at the foot of the stairs, her dark hair flying behind her.

'Daddy's going to see Mummy this evening,' she announced, prancing up the stairs in front of Miriam. 'Can I go too?'

With a shock, Miriam realized that she had forgotten to ask after the mistress of the house in the turmoil of her arrival.

'We must ask Daddy,' said she diplomatically. 'The hospital staff may not want too many visitors all at once.'

'But why not? I bet my mummy would like to see me,

and I could tell her about the toffee we made, and having bread and peanut butter for lunch today.'

By now they had traversed the long passage over the hall and Hazel flung open the door of the spare room. The light switch failed to work.

Miriam set down her heavy case and groped her way to a bedside table where she remembered that a reading lamp stood. Mercifully, it worked. Obviously, the main light needed a new bulb. She must see about that later on.

The room was cold and musty, and it was apparent that neither of the twin beds was made up. Lumpy rectangles composed of folded blankets showed through the candlewick bedspreads. She must face that job as soon as the children were in bed, and put in a hot bottle if she were to escape pneumonia in this chilly Norfolk climate. She had a strong suspicion that this room had not been used since her last visit in the early summer.

'Shall I help you unpack?' enquired Hazel, eyeing the case hopefully.

'No. I'll do it later. You run downstairs and help Daddy. I'm just coming.'

She hung up her coat on a peg on the back of the door. There was no coat-hanger to be seen in the clothes cupboard. What a house, thought Miriam! A vision of her own neat domain floated before her, and she had to wrench her mind to other matters to overcome the sudden flood of depression which engulfed her.

The bathroom was next door, chillier even than her room. The bath was grimy. The wash basin was worse, and had what looked like a used medical plaster, recently stripped from someone's damaged finger, stuck to a cracked piece of soap. Miriam gingerly picked up this

revolting amalgam and dropped it into an ancient enamel slop pail which seemed to do service as a wastepaper basket. Luckily, the bath rack provided her with a large tablet of Lifebuoy soap, and she was grateful for its disinfectant properties.

She unpacked a clean overall which she had prudently brought with her, and descended the stairs.

Lovell was slicing bread at the dresser, and Robin was sitting on the floor at his feet eating the crumbs that fell.

'Is it tea or supper?' asked Jenny.

Miriam looked at Lovell. 'As they had so light a lunch,' she said, 'what about my cooking eggs and bacon for you? And sausages if you like. Do they have a meal like that before bedtime?'

'Oh yes! Yes! We *always* have something like that, don't we?'

Their faces were rapturous. It was quite plain that they were hungry.

Lovell found her the frying pan, which was surprisingly clean, and she set about unpacking and cooking the provisions she had brought with her. Lovell, unasked, opened an enormous tin of baked beans and within twenty minutes Miriam's first meal was on the table.

There had been little culinary art in providing it and still less finesse in presenting it, straight from the pan to the waiting plates, but the children's evident relish as they demolished the meal gave her infinite satisfaction.

Now she found time to make amends and enquire after the patient.

'I'll know more when I've seen her this evening,' said Lovell. 'I'll help you to put this mob to bed and drive over to the hospital. You won't mind being left?'

'Of course not. I'll go tomorrow to see her.'

'At the moment she is under observation, I gather. She's on a pretty strict diet, and having tests. If that doesn't have any result, then they'll think of surgery.'

'What's surgery?' asked Hazel.

'It's cutting people up,' explained Jenny kindly. 'Like making chops at the butcher's.'

At this point, Robin turned his mug upside down on the tablecloth and watched the milk creep towards the edge.

'He always does that when he's finished,' said Jenny indulgently. 'Isn't he a funny boy?'

Miriam rose to fetch a dish cloth, and began to mop up the mess. Only Lovell's presence restrained her from giving a sharp reprimand to the drowsy Robin, who now leant back sucking his thumb.

The little girls watched her efforts with interest.

'We bathed Copper with that cloth this afternoon. He was smelly, so we *squeezed* it out in soapy water, and gave him a *lovely* wash.'

Miriam stopped her labours abruptly, and transferred the cloth to a battered tidy-bin beneath the sink. At this rate, she thought, a packet of 'J' cloths must take priority on tomorrow's shopping list.

'We'll wash up,' said Lovell, rising to his feet, 'and I think Robin's ready for bed if you could cope with him.'

At this, the comatose boy became instantly alert and shook his head violently.

'No! Dadda do! Dadda do!' he yelled, scarlet in the face.

'I think you'd better tonight,' said Miriam swiftly. 'He'll be more obliging when he knows me. We'll clear up here.'

The two males vanished, and Miriam and the girls set about making order out of chaos. There seemed to be a dearth of tea cloths and a decidedly vague idea of where they were kept.

'They just hang about,' said Hazel. 'On the back of that chair usually.'

'I mean the *clean* ones,' said Miriam, her voice sharp with exasperation.

'I think they're in this drawer,' said Jenny, struggling with an over-full dresser drawer stuffed with jam pot covers, pieces of string, two soup ladles and what looked like half a colander. A few pieces of tattered cloth were intermingled with debris and, after close inspection, proved to be extremely ancient tea cloths.

'Aren't you getting excited about Christmas?' enquired Jenny, patting a spoon with one of the tattered rags, as her contribution to wiping the cutlery. 'I am. I've asked Father Christmas for a painting set. Lots of different pots and brushes.'

'I hope you'll get them,' said Miriam civilly.

'Oh, she'll get them,' announced Hazel, in a meaningful way, 'but whether *Father Christmas* will bring them, I don't know.'

Jenny's face became suffused with angry colour.

'Of course he'll bring them! My letter to him went *straight* up the chimney! Yours fell back and got burnt up, and serve you right.'

'Now, now,' said Miriam warningly. Really, she thought, I sound just like my mother! How stupid 'Now, now!' sounded! Almost as idiotic as 'Now then', a phrase which could bring on partial madness if considered for too long.

It was quite apparent that Hazel was wise to the myth of Santa Claus, whilst her sister was still touchingly a believer in the Christmas fairy. She must try and get a quiet word with the older child before too much damage was done.

Lovell reappeared as they were finishing. He looked exhausted and Miriam's heart was smitten.

'Go and sit by the fire, and I'll bring you some coffee,' she said. 'You don't need to set off immediately, do you?'

'Visiting hours are seven until eight-thirty,' he said. 'Goodness, it looks clean in here! I didn't bath Robin, just washed his face and hands. He's asleep already.'

Scandalized, the little girls spoke together.

'But Robin *always* has a bath!'

'Annie *always* does him all over! He needs a bath.'

'Mummy says we *must* have a bath before bed. Robin won't like it when he wakes up and finds he's all dirty still.'

'He won't wake up,' said their father shortly.

'We'll give him an extra long one tomorrow,' promised Miriam, setting the kettle to boil, 'as it's Christmas Eve!'

When Lovell had drunk his coffee and departed, carrying Miriam's bouquet and some magazines for Eileen, she took the girls up to the bathroom and bribed them into the steaming bath with one of her precious bath cubes.

'I'll come back in ten minutes to see if you are really clean,' she told them, and left them to their own devices while she unpacked her case.

Later, scrubbed and sweet-smelling in their flowered night gowns, they held up their arms for a goodnight kiss, and Miriam admitted to herself that just now and again – for very brief periods – children could be very winning.

She descended the long staircase feeling a hundred years old. Fairacre and Holly Lodge seemed light years away. This reminded her that she had promised to ring Joan.

But not before she had revived herself with coffee, she told herself, making for the kitchen. Peremptory barking greeted her. Copper stood pointedly by his empty plate.

'Amazingly enough,' Miriam told him, 'I know where your supper is!'

She tipped out the remains of a tin of dog food she had noticed in the larder, and Copper wolfed it down with relish.

He accompanied her to the fireside when she sank into her armchair with the cup of coffee and attempted to climb on her lap.

'Some other time, Copper, old boy,' said Miriam faintly, fending him off. 'It's as much as I can do to support myself.'

She lay back and listened to the little domestic sounds of the old house. The fire whispered, a log shifted at its heart, the dog snored gently after his meal. Outside the wind stirred the trees, and somewhere a distant door banged as the breeze caught it.

Gradually, the peace that surrounded her took effect. It had been a long day, and tomorrow would be an even harder one. But meanwhile, the children slept as soundly as the dog on the rug at her feet, and the night enfolded the quiet house.

When Lovell returned, he found his sister fast asleep in the armchair.

CHAPTER SIX

M iss Quinn woke with a start, and sat bolt upright in
bed.

Close at hand a church clock was striking midnight,
and its pulsing rhythm filled the room.

Bewilderment and panic ebbed away, as she lay down
again. Of course, she was safe in her brother Lovell's
vicarage! This spare room, she remembered now, was
close to the church tower.

It must be frosty tonight to be able to hear so clearly.
Morning light would show rimy grass, no doubt, and
ice-covered puddles, the little birds huddled patiently
on sparkling twigs awaiting any bounty flung from the
kitchen.

The last stroke died away, and the old house sank back
into silence. Sleep enveloped Lovell and the three children
whom she had come to look after, over Christmas, whilst
their mother was in hospital.

Poor Eileen, she thought! Was she asleep too, or lying
awake, as she was herself? She envisaged the shadowy
ward, a night nurse sitting in the one small pool of light,
alert for any sound from a restless patient. How much
luckier she was, to be here alone and free from pain!

With a sudden shock, she realized that it was now
Christmas Eve. There would be wild excitement from
her two nieces in the next few hours. Robin would be
too young to understand, though no doubt he would be
infected by the general fever of anticipation. Did the

children hang up stockings here, she wondered, or pillow cases, as she and Lovell had done, in just such a draughty vicarage years ago?

One Christmas in particular she recalled vividly in that old Cambridgeshire house. She must have been about the same age as young Jenny asleep next door. Her milk teeth were beginning to wobble, and one in the front, she remembered, had been tipped back and forth so often by her questing tongue that her mother had begged her to 'pull it out and have done with it'. But fear had held her back, and even Lovell's pleas to 'give it a good jerk' were in vain.

Lovell, two years older, was young Miriam's hero. He could climb to the top of their yew tree, while she stuck, trembling, half-way. He could make a whistle with his pen-knife and a hollow reed. He had bloodied Billy Boston's nose when he swore about their father, and he learnt geometry at the new day school in Cambridge.

Whatever Lovell did, Miriam tried to do. Whatever Lovell told her, she believed implicitly. Whatever Lovell said was right was so, and whatever Lovell found wrong was, of course, quite wrong.

That particular Christmas Miriam was much exercised in her mind. Ruby, her six-year-old friend at school, had stated categorically that there was no Father Christmas. Miriam was horrified at such an infamous statement.

'Of course there is! You get presents, don't you?'

Ruby, skipping busily at the time, was offhand.

'Your mum or dad puts 'em there,' she puffed, twirling the rope.

'I don't believe it,' said Miriam stoutly, but a cold hand seemed to clutch at her stomach. Could it be true? Could her father and mother have told her lies? Could Lovell?

Never, she told herself! Lovell always told her the truth. If there were no Father Christmases, Lovell would have said so. It was Ruby who told lies.

'You don't know what you're talking about,' she told the skipper robustly. 'I just *know* there's a Father Christmas, so there!'

'Better stay awake and find out,' shouted Ruby to Miriam who was walking away.

And maybe I will, thought Miriam, stubbornly, just to prove she's wrong.

In the few days left before Christmas she often asked her mother about this problem. But, as always, the vicarage was fast filling up with elderly relatives who were coming to spend Christmas with the family, and Mrs Quinn was busy with preparations.

Nevertheless, both parents replied kindly to Miriam's tentative enquiries about the authenticity of Father Christmas, but were vague and preoccupied. On the whole though, she felt slightly reassured.

Among the Christmas guests was a recently-widowed young aunt with her four-year-old son, Sidney. The child was delicate, and made even more so by his mother's molly-coddling.

'Naturally she fusses over him,' Miriam heard her mother say to one of the elderly second cousins. 'He's all she has now, and he is a dear little boy.'

Lovell and Miriam did not think so. They thought him spoilt, a cry-baby and a tale-teller. The fact that the poor child lisped, only made him more ridiculous in their eyes. With childish heartlessness they teased the little boy, without mercy, whenever they had him alone.

It so happened that this particular Christmas Eve

brought snow to bleak East Anglia, and the three children were wrapped up warmly and sent to play, with injunctions to make a snowman. Lovell and Miriam, strong and boisterous, threw themselves into the task joyfully, but Sidney, half-afraid of the bigger children and disliking the cold, did little.

'Come on, Thid,' shouted Lovell, 'lend a hand!'

'Thid, Thid, Thilly-Thid-Thid!' mocked Miriam, following Lovell's lead as usual.

The child shook his head unhappily, near to tears. Irritated by his apathy, the two young savages began to chase him round and round the half-built snowman. Within two minutes the little boy was sobbing, and struggling to escape from his tormentors. They pursued him ruthlessly, until at last he fell wailing into the snowman

and the bigger children, incensed at the damage, rolled the child back and forth in the snow.

'Now look what you've done!'

'All our work spoilt! We'll pay you out for this!'

They began stuffing snow down the neck of the child's jersey, giggling now, but still enjoying the feeling of power over this weakling.

Sidney's cries attracted his mother. The three children were driven into the kitchen and the young Quinns were accused by Sidney's hysterical mother of gross cruelty. Mrs Quinn banished her two to their bedrooms for an hour, after apologies all round, and Miriam spent the time wobbling the front tooth and thinking about the existence, or otherwise, of Father Christmas.

Called down to tea after their penance, Miriam spoke urgently to Lovell as they went into the dining-room.

'Ruby Adair at school said there wasn't a Father Christmas. Is it true?'

An extraordinary look came over Lovell's face. It was as though Miriam had hit him. He stuttered when he replied, a thing he only did when very upset.

'You don't want to believe everything Ruby says,' he managed to say. 'I've never told you that, have I?'

The tension, which had screwed Miriam's inside into a painful knot, lessened at once, and the feeling of relief carried her through the hours until bedtime. She even managed to speak kindly to the loathsome Sidney who insisted on sitting close to his mother.

Bedtime came. The three children prepared the traditional snack for Father Christmas, a mince pie from each one, and a glass of orange squash which Sidney chose as the best drink available.

Miriam watched Lovell closely as they placed the food in the hearth. His face was solemn, and he was being uncommonly gentle with young Sidney. He would not take such trouble, thought Miriam with relief, if he did not truly expect Father Christmas to arrive.

The children went to bed. Over each bed rail hung an empty pillow case. Miriam looked at hers as she lay awake. If, as silly Ruby said, one's parents filled it, then she would be bound to hear them.

Despite her intention to stay alert, she was asleep in ten minutes. The sound of the door opening woke her, hours later.

'All right?' she heard her mother whisper.

Her father answered: 'Fast asleep!'

Cold with horror, she lay motionless.

She saw the empty pillow case twitched from the bed rail, and felt the bump of a full one as it was lodged at the foot of the bed. So *that* was how it was done!

The door closed noiselessly. She lay there, numbed with shock. A painful lump swelled in her throat, and hot tears began to trickle. Ruby was right.

To think that all this time her parents had lied! And Lovell too! It was cruel. All these years she had loved Father Christmas, and now it was spoilt.

She crept from her bed, and squatting on the floor, she felt the various shapes in the pillow case. There was the doll she had asked for, and this box must be the tea-set or a jigsaw puzzle. She could smell the fragrance of the tangerine tucked in a corner, and could hear the rattle of the nuts in the other.

Tears continued to course down her cheeks. She would

not unpack things until morning light. And would she enjoy them then, she wondered, knowing that Lovell had betrayed her? Would things ever be the same again?

Her feet were cold as stones, and she clambered back into bed. As she did so, her restless tongue finally broke the loose tooth from its precarious moorings. Still weeping, she felt the edge of the new tooth thrusting through. She pulled the clothes about her, and fell into an uneasy sleep.

Leaden-eyed and leaden-hearted next morning, she did her best to share in the general excitement.

At the breakfast table she thanked all her relatives for their gifts. She could hardly bear to look at Lovell, so happy and unconcerned.

Sidney was flushed with joy and excitement.

'All gone!' he said, showing her Father Christmas's empty plate. 'Did you thee him?'

He pressed against Miriam anxiously.

'Did you thee him?' he persisted.

Conscious of the eyes of all upon her, her heart raging with bitterness, Miriam took a deep breath. She turned her blazing gaze upon the traitor Lovell.

'No, I *didn't*,' she burst forth. 'I *didn't* see Father Christmas, Sidney. But I'll tell you what I *did* see!'

The child looked up at her, smiling and trusting.

Lovell's gaze was steady. Across the breakfast table, brother and sister were locked in a look.

Very slowly Lovell shook his head. Briefly, and with a wealth of meaning, he glanced at Sidney, and then looked back at Miriam. It was a conspiratorial look, and it filled Miriam's quivering body with warmth and comfort. Now, in a flash, she understood. Suddenly, she was grown up. Hadn't she felt the first of her adult teeth this very morning?

A little child, as she had been until now, had the right to believe in this magic. She felt suddenly protective towards the young boy beside her. She, and Lovell, and all the other people present, knew, and faced the responsibilities of knowing, this precious secret. Now, she too was one of the elect.

'What did you thee?' asked Sidney.

'I saw the door closing,' said Miriam. 'That's all.'

Across the table, Lovell smiled at her with approval. Her heart leapt, and Christmas Day became again the joyful festival she had always known.

How sharply it came back, thought Miss Quinn, that memory of thirty years ago! The shock of her enlightenment was some measure of the joy she had formerly felt in the myth of Father Christmas. She was glad that Jenny and Robin were still ardent believers, and she must try and make sure that Hazel, on the brink of knowledge, did not suffer as she had done as a child, and did not tarnish the glitter for the younger ones.

Somewhere, in some distant copse, a fox gave an eerie cry.

The scudding clouds parted briefly, and a shaft of moonlight fell across the bed.

The night was made for sleeping, said Miriam to herself, and tomorrow there was much to be done. There were children to be tended, Eileen to visit, provisions to organize, and all to be accomplished amidst the joyous frenzy of Christmas Eve.

Resolutely, she applied herself to sleep.

CHAPTER SEVEN

She awoke, much refreshed, still with the memories of past Christmas times about her, and determined to make the present one happy for the children.

It was still dark, but she could hear children's voices. Perhaps they were already up? She put her warm feet upon the chilly linoleum and went to the door. The house felt icy.

Sure enough, the two little girls were scampering about the long passage half-dressed. They greeted her with cries of joy, and bounced into her room unbidden. Wails from Robin could be heard in the distance.

'Oh, he's all right,' said Hazel casually. 'Daddy's put him on his potty, and he doesn't want to go. That's all.'

Jenny was fingering Miriam's hair brush.

'I've asked Father Christmas for one like this,' she said.

Hazel's lip began to curl in a derisory manner, and Miriam, recalling her night-time memory, put a hand on her arm. There was no mistaking the alert glance that the child flashed at her. She knew all right!

Remembering Lovell's meaningful shake of the head so long ago, she repeated the small gesture to his daughter. The child half-smiled in return, squeezed the restraining hand upon her arm, and remained silent.

That, thought Miriam, thankfully, was one hurdle surmounted!

'What do you have for breakfast?' she enquired, tactfully changing the subject.

'Cornflakes, or shredded wheat,' said Hazel.

'Sometimes toast, if there's time,' said Jenny.

'What does Daddy have?' asked Miriam, secretly thinking that Eileen should surely cook a breakfast, if not for the children, then for a man off to his parish duties in the coldest part of England.

'The same,' they chorused.

'Go and get dressed,' said Miriam, 'and I'll make toast for us all, and perhaps a boiled egg.'

'Oh, lovely!' squealed the children. 'Let's go and tell Robin!'

They fled, leaving Miriam to have the bathroom in peace.

At breakfast, Miriam broached the practical problem of catering for the household for four days. The basic things seemed to be in the house, and she knew that there were Brussels sprouts, cabbages and carrots in the vegetable garden.

A Christmas pudding stood on the pantry shelf, but she would have to make mince pies and other sweets and where was the turkey – or was it to be a round of beef?

Lovell was vague. He rather thought a friend of theirs was supplying the turkey, but he would have imagined it would have been delivered by now.

'Will it be dressed?' asked Miriam, with considerable anxiety. She might be Sir Barnabas's right hand, but she knew her limits. Drawing a fowl was not among her talents.

'Dressed?' queried Hazel, egg-spoon arrested half-way to her mouth. 'What in?'

Gales of giggles greeted this sally.

'A bonnet,' gasped Jenny, 'and shawl! Like Jemima Puddleduck. That's what turkeys dress in!'

The two little girls rolled about in paroxysms of mirth. Lovell cast his eyes heavenward, in mock disdain.

'Dressed means ready to put in the oven,' explained Miriam, laughing.

'I know a boy at school who can pull out the tubes and smelly bits,' said Hazel, recovering slightly. 'Is that what you mean?'

'Exactly,' said Miriam.

At that moment the telephone rang, and Lovell vanished.

'It might still have its feathers on,' remarked Jenny.

'And it's head,' added Hazel.

Miriam's qualms intensified.

'How do you get its head off?' enquired Jenny conversationally, scraping the last of her egg from the shell.

Miriam was spared replying as Lovell returned.

'The chairman of Eileen's bench. Just enquiring.'

Eileen, she remembered now, had recently been made a magistrate. Frankly she wondered if she were capable of the task, but simply said politely: 'Does she worry much about her duties?'

'What she really worries about,' replied Lovell, 'is whether she should wear a hat or not.'

Then, sensing that this might smack of disloyalty, he enlarged on the many compliments he had heard from her fellows on the bench, on Eileen's good sense and fair-mindedness.

His discourse was cut short by a ring at the back door. Hazel skipped off to answer it and came back, much excited.

'It's the turkey man, Aunt Miriam, and it's all right! He's bare!'

Construing this correctly, Miriam felt a wave of relief, and hurried to fetch the bird, Lovell following close behind to pay the bill.

A little later, she sallied forth with several baskets, and the three children in tow. Lovell had to conduct a funeral service and visit two desperately sick parishioners. He would be back to late lunch, and then stay at the vicarage while Miriam visited the hospital.

'Can you possibly get back by about four, do you think?' he enquired, consulting a list anxiously. 'I'm supposed to call at the village hall to have tea with the Over-Sixty Club, and be at a Brownies' Carol Service in the next parish at the same time. Then I must have a word with the flower ladies, and get ready for the midnight service.'

Miriam assured him that she could manage easily.

'Can we come and see Mummy?'

'Yes, can we?' clamoured the girls. Miriam looked at Lovell.

'Sister made no objection last time, as long as they behave, of course, and aren't there too long. But how do you feel?'

'I'd like their company,' said Miriam, and they fell upon her with shrieks of joy.

The grocer's shop was one of three in the village. Across the road was the butcher's, and next door was the Post Office which sold sweets and tobacco.

The proprietor of the village stores bore a strong resemblance to Mrs Pringle of Fairacre. She had the same square frame, the identical short cropped hair and an expression of malevolent resignation.

Fortunately, the similarity ended there, and she turned out to be unusually helpful about the needs of the vicarage household.

'Did you want the piece of gammon Mrs Quinn asked about? I've put it by, in case.'

'Yes, please,' said Miriam. At least it would make a change from turkey in the days to come.

'And you'll want potatoes,' Mrs Bates informed her. 'That half-hundred-weight was nearly finished last week, Annie told me.'

Miriam, slightly dazed, remembered that Eileen's mother's help was a local girl.

'I'm her auntie,' vouchsafed Mrs Bates, scrabbling in a box of potatoes hidden behind the counter. Fairacre all over again, thought Miriam!

'Take five pounds now, and my Bert'll bring up ten pounds later if that suits you. You don't want to hump all that lot, and Robin's push-chair's not that strong.'

Miriam agreed meekly. It was quite a change to be managed. Was this how Barney felt when she mapped out his routine?

With a shock she remembered there had been no preparations made for lunch at home. For the first time in her life, she bought fish fingers, and a ready made blackcurrant tart. How often she had watched scornfully the feckless mothers buying expensive 'convenience' foods. Now, with three children distracting her, and the clock ticking on inexorably, she sympathized with them. Catering for one, she began to realize, was quite a different

matter from trying to please the varying tastes of five people, and hungry ones at that.

'Where's Robin?' she enquired suddenly. The child had vanished.

Hazel and Jenny were talking to a boy in the doorway.

'Probably in the road,' said Mrs Bates. 'And the traffic's something awful this morning.'

There was a hint of mournful satisfaction in this remark that reminded Miriam yet again of the distant Mrs Pringle.

She rushed to the door, heart thudding, calling his name. The road was clear, except for a scrawny dog carrying a large bone.

'It's all right!' shouted Mrs Bates behind her. 'He's here.'

The child was sitting on the floor, hidden behind the end of the counter, beside a rolled-down sack containing dog biscuits which he was eating with the voracity of one just released from a concentration camp.

'Robin, *really*!' exclaimed his aunt. Like Tabitha Twitchit, she thought suddenly, I am affronted.

'Don't worry, miss. He's partial to dog biscuits. And these are extra pure,' she added virtuously.

'You must let me pay you,' said Miriam, hauling the child to his feet and brushing yellow sulphur biscuit crumbs from his coat.

'Oh, he's welcome,' said Mrs Bates indulgently. 'I'll just add up the other.'

By the time she had visited the butcher, to buy steak and kidney for a casserole for the evening meal, and then the Post Office for stamps and sweets, Miriam seemed to have accumulated three heavy baskets.

The wind was now boisterous, and carrying rain bordering on sleet. The children did not seem to notice the cold, but Miriam, struggling with the erratic push-chair and the shopping, felt frozen through.

Ah! Dear Holly Lodge, she thought with longing! Tucked into the shelter of the downs, screened by that stout hedge, when would she see it again?

'What a lovely, lovely lunch,' sighed Jenny, leaning back replete.

'Excellent!' agreed her father.

Miriam was secretly amused. If her friends could have seen the meal she had assembled, fish fingers, instant potatoes, tinned beans and bottled tomato sauce, followed by the bought fruit pie, her standing as a first-class cook would have taken a jolt.

And yet it had been relished. Perhaps there was a moral here, but there was certainly no time to pursue the thought, with the washing-up to be done, the girls to get ready, and Robin to be put down for his afternoon nap. She must put the steak and kidney in a slow oven too, so that it would cook gently while they were at the hospital. How on earth did mothers manage? She was more exhausted now, at midday, than she was at the end of a hard week at the office.

At half past two she set out, with the girls in a state of wild excitement in the back of the car. They were carrying their Christmas presents for Eileen, and keeping an eye on Miriam's. Tomorrow Lovell would be the only visitor at the hospital, while Miriam took charge at home.

Eileen looked prettier and younger than ever, propped against her pillows in a frilly pale blue nightgown. It so happened that Miriam's present was also a nightgown, but a black chiffon one threaded with narrow black satin ribbon. It would make a splendid contrast, she thought, to the one she was now wearing.

Eileen greeted them all with hugs and kisses.

'You are a perfect angel to come to our rescue,' she said when the little girls had been settled, in comparative peace, with some magazines. 'Have you had a terrible time coping?'

Miriam reassured her.

'I think all the shopping's done. No doubt I've forgotten something quite vital like bread, but I've remembered stuffing for the bird and even salted peanuts in case people come in for drinks.'

'That's more than I should have done,' said Eileen
cheerfully, and Miriam began to feel more drawn to her
sister-in-law than ever before. There was something
engaging about such candour.

'Is that lady dying?' asked Jenny, in a high carrying
voice, her finger pointing to a grey-faced woman dozing
in the next bed. Miriam went cold with shock.

Eileen laughed merrily.

'Good heavens, no! Mrs White is getting better faster
than any of us. Be very quiet, darling, so that she doesn't
wake up.'

At this point, Sister arrived, and asked Eileen if the
children would like to see the Christmas tree in the
children's ward. They departed happily.

'By the way,' said Miriam, 'did you know that Hazel
has tumbled to Father Christmas?'

'Yes. I hope she won't tell Jenny yet.'

Miriam explained what had happened.

'Always problems,' said Eileen. 'And with some you will be wrong whatever you do. I thought this when Lovell and I were invited out together, the other evening. He was suddenly taken ill. Of course I rang our hostess, and she said; "Will you feel like coming?" What do you do? Say "Yes" and be branded as callous to one's husband's sufferings, and probably greedy to boot, or say "No" and let down the hostess?'

'Insoluble,' agreed Miriam. 'Or, worse still, wondering whether to pull the lavatory chain, in the dead of night, in someone else's house. If you do, you can imagine the startled hostess saying: "You'd think she would have more sense than to rouse the whole household!" On the other hand, one is liable to be branded a perfect slut if the hostess visits the loo first in the morning!'

They laughed together, and Miriam, for the first time, felt completely at ease in Eileen's presence.

'But tell me about yourself,' she said. 'Are they getting things right?'

'I think so. They couldn't be kinder, and once the results of the tests are through I may be able to come home. Strict diet, and all that, and weekly check-ups, but I've a strong suspicion it won't come to surgery.'

'Thank God for that!' said Miriam.

'You must be longing to get back to Fairacre,' said Eileen. 'The vicarage is such a barn of a place. But Lovell is terribly grateful to you for coming up so quickly, and so am I, as you know. We should have foundered without you. Ah, here comes Sister.'

The children had been given a chocolate toy from the tree, and were starry-eyed with pleasure.

'Shall I unwrap your presents while you're here?' asked Eileen.

'Yes, yes. Do it now!' they clamoured.

With great care, she undid the wrappings, read the lop-sided cards covered in kiss-crosses, and finally displayed a canvas book mark embroidered in lazy-daisy-stitch by Hazel, and a thimble in a walnut-shell case from Jenny.

'Perfect!' smiled Eileen, putting the thimble on her finger, and the bookmark in the novel by her bed. 'Now Christmas has really begun!'

Miriam looked at her watch.

'I must take them back. Lovell has to be off again by four. He'll be in tomorrow, and I'll come again after that.'

'Dear Miriam,' murmured Eileen, as they kissed. 'No wonder Lovell adores you. You are an absolute tower of strength.'

Miriam called into Sister's room, as they went out, to thank her for the children's presents, and to enquire after Eileen's progress.

'She's doing very well. We couldn't have a better patient, and a real help to the others in the ward.'

'She says you are all very good to her.'

'That's nothing to Mr Quinn's kindness to my old mother,' said Sister, with energy. 'You don't forget help like that when you're in trouble. He lives by his beliefs, that brother of yours.'

'He tries to, I know,' replied Miriam, much moved.

'Come on, Aunt Miriam, we've got to get our things ready for Father Christmas,' urged the girls.

'First things first,' called Sister, as they left the hospital.

*

The wind had become a vicious howling gale by the time they reached home. The sleet slanted across the headlights, and a wicked draught blew from the east under the vicarage doors. Water was blowing out to the landing, from a window which took the brunt of the weather, and Miriam searched for something to staunch the flow.

'Mummy just leaves it,' said Jenny, faintly surprised at so much fuss over some intruding rain. 'It always dries up after a bit.'

Exhausted as she was, Miriam began to sympathize with this *laissez-faire* attitude, although it was against all her principles. She rammed a shabby towel against the crack, and hoped for the best.

Lovell had departed into the waste of wind and water, and Robin's bathtime arrived. Hazel and Jenny accompanied her to the bathroom, anxious to help and to explain to the boy the importance of hanging up his stocking.

Less hostile than the previous evening, nevertheless the child still resented Miriam's attention.

'Dadda do!' he muttered sulkily. 'Go away!'

'You're a bad boy,' scolded Hazel, 'to say that to Aunt Miriam when she's come all this way to look after you!'

Robin responded by blowing a mouthful of soapy water over his sister. Most of it went on Miriam's skirt.

Jenny improved the shining hour by telling the child about Father Christmas.

'And he'll creep in to your room, in a red coat,' she began, but was interrupted by a fearful screeching from her brother.

'No want! No want!' he screamed, shaking his head violently.

Jenny looked resignedly at Miriam who was doing her best to soap his thrashing legs.

'You know, he's frightened, that's what! He's just *frightened* of Father Christmas. What'll we do?'

Hazel came to the rescue.

'Put his stocking on the banisters, then he'll be all right, won't he?'

She looked at Miriam with a conspiratorial glance.

'Good idea,' she said hastily, praying that the secret would still be kept.

She hauled the boy out of the water, amidst more shrieking, and muffled his cries in a warm towel. The bathroom, steamy and damp, was the warmest place in the house, and she was loath to leave it to put the child into his cot in the chilly bedroom. What this place needs, she told herself, and will never get, is a thoroughly efficient central-heating system.

The two little girls had climbed into the bath together, lured into an early bedtime by the promise of supper by the fire downstairs, and the happy prospect of hanging up stockings.

Miriam left them there while she warmed their milk in the kitchen. Outside, the rain lashed at the window, and the branches of the apple tree creaked and groaned. A particularly fierce draught under the larder door made a noise like a banshee wailing. This was Norfolk at its worst, thought Miriam, but at least the stove was warm, and the comforting smell of the steak casserole counteracted the bleakness outside.

The sitting-room was snug with the curtains drawn and the fire blazing. The two little girls nursed their bowls of cornflakes liberally topped with brown sugar and raisins, and asked Miriam to tell them about Christmas when she was small.

'Well,' began Miriam, 'we used to hang up pillow cases, your daddy and I.'

'So do we. And stockings.'

'And we left a mince-pie and some milk for Father Christmas, in the hearth.'

'So do we,' they chorused.

'And after he'd been,' said Miriam, looking squarely at Hazel, whose face remained rapt, 'we took our pillow cases into grandma and grandpa's bed and undid all our parcels.'

'And what did you have?'

Miriam suddenly remembered the agonizing night when she felt her parcels as the tears rolled down her cheeks. She could taste them now, salty and bitter, and feel the lump in her aching throat.

'Are you all right?' asked Hazel.

'Yes, just thinking,' said Miriam. 'Oh, a doll, and a tea set with little flowers on it, and, of course, a tangerine and nuts and sweets. Lots of lovely things.' And heartbreak, she added silently. God, that heartbreak! Nothing in her adult life had ever hurt quite so piercingly.

'Can we bring our things into your bedroom?' asked Jenny, spooning up the last drop.

'Of course you can!' cried Miriam. 'On Christmas Day you can do anything you like! Within reason,' she added prudently.

They skipped upstairs before her, and accompanied her to the linen cupboard for two pillowcases. A pair of Eileen's stockings already hung over their bed rail.

'Do you think they'll be full?' asked Jenny.

'Positively brimming over,' Miriam promised her, tucking them in, and praying that sleep would soon engulf them.

Later that evening, she and Lovell drowsed before the fire, before he went over to the church for his late service. In her lap billowed the great black mass of Lovell's cassock.

'Must have caught my heel in the hem,' he said apologetically, as he handed it over. 'Do you mind?'

She now stitched languidly, thinking yet again how many varied tasks fell to the lot of a married woman.

'I wish I could have found someone else to do it – and to help you in the house,' said Lovell. 'But everyone's so busy at Christmas time. Looking back, I realize how lucky we were at home to have dear old Euphrosyne and her like, coping in the kitchen. It meant Mother had the energy needed to cope with parish affairs.'

'From what I hear,' said Miriam, snipping black cotton, 'Eileen does very well.'

'She has to do far too much,' sighed Lovell. 'How did she look today?'

'Ravishing as ever,' said Miriam, and told him about her visit, and Sister's kindness, and her remark about his own.

Lovell looked surprised.

'Really? I did nothing you know. Just called now and again.'

'And she also said that Eileen was a marvellous patient and a great help in the ward.'

His face softened.

'She's the bravest person I know. She's been so sweet

with that poor woman in the next bed. A terminal case, they call it. She wasn't expected to live through the night.'

Miriam remembered her niece's query, her own horror, and Eileen's courageous laughter. There was certainly more to this sister-in-law of hers than she had ever imagined.

'Well, there you are,' she said, shaking out the cassock. 'I shall wait up for you, and we'll have the fun of filling the pillowcases together.'

'You shouldn't. You look whacked, so don't stay up just for me.'

He shrugged into the cassock, threw his coat over his shoulders and made for the door.

'I shall be back soon after one, I expect,' he shouted above the wind, waved, and was gone.

Miriam was about to return to the fireside when she remembered that she had intended to stuff the turkey and prepare some of the vegetables for the morrow.

Should she go into the kitchen and tackle these chores? Or should she give way to temptation and collapse into the armchair?

Bravely, she made her way towards the larder, follow-ed by Copper, ever-anxious for a meal.

'And to think,' she told the dog, 'that I'm known as a working woman. I wonder what Eileen is?'

CHAPTER EIGHT

The day began, in pitch darkness, at five-thirty.

Miriam's door opened, and Hazel and Jenny entered dragging their spoils behind them.

'You said we could come,' beamed Hazel.

'And you said we could do anything we liked on Christmas Day, so here we are!'

Miriam sat up and switched on the bedside lamp. Her head was heavy with sleep, her eyes felt as though they were full of biscuit crumbs. But this was Christmas morning, and although it had come far too soon for comfort, Christian feelings must predominate.

'Happy Christmas, darlings,' she said, between yawns. 'Switch on the electric fire, Hazel, and both come into bed. You must be frozen.'

They joyously flung their laden pillow cases on to their aunt's stomach, partially winding her. Their bare feet were like four ice-blocks pressed against her own warm legs. Their hands, diving for their treasures were mottled with the cold.

'Where's Robin?' asked Miriam.

'Still asleep. So's Daddy. Shall we go and fetch them?'

'No, no. They'll come along later. Let's see all these gorgeous things.'

She duly admired books, jigsaw puzzles, and a complicated board game which she feared would be beyond her when the time came for it to be played.

There were recorders, played with more enthusiasm

than harmony, dolls and their clothes – remarkably sophisticated to Miriam's eye. No doll of hers ever had ski clothes, bathing dresses, or evening cloaks. These beauties even had handbags to match their different outfits. The girls were enchanted.

Miriam had given Hazel a toy sewing machine, and Jenny a little cooking stove. She was relieved to see how ecstatically these were received, and promised to help them when they started to use them.

'I shall make tiny, tiny, dear little chips and fry them in this frying pan,' cried Jenny. 'You can have some for supper.'

Miriam lay back on her pillow and watched them affectionately. Everything enchanted them, even the two plain aprons sent by a distant great-aunt. It was good to see such unspoilt children. Lovell and Eileen had done a good job with these two, thought their aunt proudly.

She looked about the room, which was now beginning to get warm The children had hung a red paper bell over the door, when they had decorated the house with all the Christmas paper chains, folding fans and other ornaments earlier in the week. It really looked rather pretty, thought Miriam, remembering how she and Lovell had always adored unfolding these showy decorations as children to deck the old Fenland vicarage. What would these children think of her own bare quarters at Holly Lodge if they could see them?

But something indefinable was missing. Was it the smell of tangerines?

Before she could pin it down, Lovell came in carrying Robin with his stocking.

'Merry Christmas!' they all shouted.

'It's marvellously warm in here,' said Lovell. 'Reminds me of Christmas morning at home when we used to have the Valor Perfection stove alight in the bedroom.'

'That's it!' cried Miriam. 'I've been missing the smell of paraffin!'

'And a good thing too, I should think,' said Lovell, helping his youngest to unwrap a furry panda.

'But it was heavenly in the dark,' remembered Miriam, 'making lovely patterns on the ceiling.'

'And lovely smuts when it smoked,' added Lovell.

The little girls were busily opening their brother's presents and urging him to admire them. Robin appeared to be as sleepy as Miriam felt herself, and greeted each discovery with a marked lack of enthusiasm.

'What we need,' said Miriam, when the last parcel was

undone, and the bedroom floor was awash with Christmas wrappings, 'is an early breakfast. And then you can play with your new toys before we go to church.'

Lovell had a service at eight, and Miriam proposed to take the children to the eleven o'clock service, bringing them out before the sermon.

'But you can't leave the *turkey*,' protested Hazel, as though it were an invalid aunt in need of constant care.

'I can, you know,' said Miriam. 'You'll see.'

'I could cook something on my stove,' said Jenny. 'Peas, say.'

'There'd only be a mouthful,' said Hazel.

'I could *keep on* cooking peas,' replied Jenny snappily. 'Then there'd be enough. Fish shops *keep on* cooking, don't they, Aunt Miriam? Everyone has enough.'

By mid-morning tempers were beginning to fray. After such an early awakening, and now that the toys had been inspected, the children started to quarrel.

It was the first time that Miriam had seen the two sisters at war, and she was staggered at the ferocity of the battle. She was at a loss too, to know how best to quell this uprising.

Robin, more animated than he had yet appeared, looked on the scene with approval, clapping his hands as Jenny clutched her sister's long hair and attempted to haul it from her scalp.

Hazel retaliated with a resounding smack on Jenny's cheek. Screams rent the air, and Miriam rushed to part them. This was something entirely new to her. Once, she remembered, she had been called to a couple in the typing room at the office who had reduced each other to tears over some business about a boyfriend. That had been bad enough, but this was real commando stuff.

A sharp scratch from Hazel's finger nail caused her such sudden pain that involuntarily she smacked the child's arm, and Jenny's too. The manoeuvre worked like a charm, both fell apart, open mouthed with astonishment.

'Mummy *never, never* hits us!' exclaimed Hazel, much shocked.

'Nor Daddy,' cried Jenny, coming to her late enemy's support.

The words: 'More fool them,' hovered on Miriam's lips, but she forbore to utter them. She was still suffering from pain, shock and some shame at the violence of her reaction.

'You can go upstairs, and get ready for church,' she said instead. 'And no more nonsense!'

They went out quietly, but before they had reached the stairs Miriam heard them giggling together, all conflict over.

An ominous pattering noise, attracted her attention. Robin was inspecting a growing puddle on the kitchen floor.

'Good boy!' he said approvingly. 'Good boy, Robin.'

Sighing, Miriam went in search of a bucket and floor cloth.

An hour later, she and her charges sat decorously in church awaiting Lovell's entrance.

The building was plain, with only a few mural tablets bearing testimony to the virtues of the deceased and the grief of those mourning them. A threadbare banner hung from one wall, a reminder of the gallantry of an East Anglian regiment and

> *Old unhappy far-off things*
> *And battles long ago.*

The church was half full, which Miriam rightly construed as a good congregation. She had attended a service here with only three other worshippers, on one occasion.

The organ swelled into a recognizable tune, and the congregation rose as the choir entered, followed by Lovell.

'That's my Daddy!' cried Robin joyously, much to the delight of nearby worshippers. Jenny and Hazel shook their heads with disapproval, but were obviously secretly proud of their brother's intelligence.

The service began, but its measured beauty failed to hold Miriam's attention, distracted as she was by having to find the place for the two little girls, and by restraining Robin who was busy licking the varnished pew shelf, as though it were made of butterscotch, which it somewhat resembled.

This activity was accompanied by loud smacking noises and an appreciative growling such as puppies make when enjoying a bone. Miriam's efforts to divert him were met with vociferous resistance, and a renewed attack upon the woodwork. A particularly solemn silence, at the end of one of the prayers, was broken by a crunching sound. Robin, raising his head to admire his toothwork, turned, dribbling heavily, to Miriam, and patted the wet shelf encouragingly.

'Auntie bite!' he demanded. 'Auntie bite too!'

'No!' hissed Miriam fiercely. Really, to think that a two-year-old could cause so much embarrassment! She was conscious of considerable merriment in the pews behind her. Should she take the child out, she wondered?

Luckily, at this juncture they all stood for the hymn preceding the sermon.

'Do we put our money in now?' enquired Hazel loudly. 'Because I've lost mine.'

Jenny, with sisterly concern, fell to the floor and began searching busily along a very dusty heating pipe.

'P'raps it's rolled under the seat,' she suggested, pointing with a black hand. Hazel bent down, as though about to join her in the depths.

'Leave it,' begged Miriam helplessly. 'I will give you some more.'

'But we *can't* just leave it!' protested Jenny. By now her face was striped with grime. She looked like a very cross tiger cub.

'It's not now anyway,' responded Jenny. 'It's the next

hymn we put the money in. Daddy does his talking, and then we put it in, don't we, Aunt Miriam?'

'Well, we won't be here then,' argued Hazel, 'so what shall we do with our money? Aunt Miriam, we don't want any collection money, so can we keep it?'

Powerless to check this flow of conversation, Miriam saw, with infinite relief, that Lovell was ascending the stairs to the pulpit. This was her cue to remove his lively offspring.

She began to usher the children into the aisle. Fortunately, she had purposely taken a pew near to the door. Robin resisted strongly, and appealed to the distant figure in the pulpit.

'Dadda!' he screamed lustily. 'Dadda do! Dadda do!'

The two little girls contented themselves with waving cheerfully as they made for the door, but Robin sat suddenly in the aisle and refused to budge.

An elderly sidesman, seeing Miriam's dilemma, advanced and picked up the boy, who made himself as stiff as a board, whilst keeping up a barrage of ear-splitting yells.

He was borne towards the door, Miriam following. She gave one apologetic backward glance towards Lovell. His dark face was impassive, but there was a gleam in his eye which told her clearly of his enjoyment of the scene.

'Like a sweet?' said the sidesman to Robin, when they gained the porch. The screams stopped abruptly.

He deposited the boy on the gravel path outside and felt in his waistcoat pocket. Hazel and Jenny watched with attention.

He produced three small fruit drops each wrapped in cellophane, and handed them down.

'Always as well to have sweets on you when there are children around,' he said kindly to Miriam, and departed before she had time to thank him properly.

It was wonderful to be out in the air again. The wind was still strong, but the rain had gone, and now the scudding clouds parted, and the sun lit up the wide Norfolk fields around the flint church.

'I *love* Christmas,' said Jenny, cheek bulging. 'Do you?'

Miriam looked at the three children, so quickly transformed into angels.

'Yes,' she said. 'I do.'

The turkey which had been left to its own devices in the oven, much to the concern of the two little girls, had assumed a luscious golden brown when Miriam returned to baste it.

She put on the vegetables and topped up the water in the steamer holding the Christmas pudding before going to set the table.

She had ransacked the airing cupboard and at last had found a large white damask cloth, old and beautifully starched, with several darns executed, she guessed, by a long-dead hand. No one these days, surely, could be bothered to do such fine work.

Spread upon the dining-room table and decorated with two candlesticks borrowed from the mantelpiece, it began to look more like a festive board, although Miriam cursed herself for forgetting to buy crackers, those instant decorations. As it was, there was no time to search for flowers or ribbons, but she filched a few holly sprigs from above the pictures where the children had put them, and set them round the candlesticks.

'It's *marvellous*!' cried Hazel.

'Can we put some pretty things on too?' queried Jenny.

'Yes, do,' said Miriam, rushing to the kitchen to attend to an ominous hissing noise.

When she returned, she found that Hazel had added a small sleigh holding Father Christmas and bath cubes, an inspired present from an aunt in America, whilst Jenny had purloined the fairy from the top of the Christmas tree to add to the scene.

Robin's contribution was a toy camel with three lead legs and one of plasticine. It added an exotic touch as it leant, in a drunken fashion, against a candlestick.

Lovell admired everything warmly when he returned from church, and the meal was as cheerful as he and Miriam could make it for the children.

Afterwards, the two adults dozed while Robin slept upstairs and the two little girls played with their new toys. A walk was planned for three o'clock, but when the time came Miriam saw that Lovell was still deep in sleep. Now she observed how tired he looked, how the lines had deepened in his face and how his dark hair was showing flecks of grey. His work and Eileen's illness were taking their toll of his energy, and she grieved for him.

Quietly, she slipped from the room and summoned Hazel and Jenny. A look into Robin's room showed the boy as deep in slumber as his father.

'We'll play games at the end of the garden,' said Miriam, 'instead of going for a walk. Then we can be near Robin if he wakes.'

'Goody-goody-gum-drops!' cried Jenny. 'We'll have longer with our toys then.'

The kitchen garden was a vast area with a mellowed

brick and flint wall. A hundred years or so earlier it must have been the pride of a head gardener and probably two or three under-gardeners. Now it sheltered only a few rows of Brussels sprouts, carrots and cabbages, but it afforded a playground out of the wind and far enough away from the house for the children's shouts to be unheard.

Miriam showed them how to play two-ball against the wall and was surprised and proud to find that she had not lost her skill over the years. After initial difficulties, the girls soon became quite dextrous, the only snag being that only two balls could be found, and they had to take it in turns.

'As soon as the shops open,' promised Miriam, 'I'll buy you two new ones each.'

'But that's not till Monday,' wailed Hazel. 'It's ages away!'

'*What can't be cured must be endured,*' Miriam said cheerfully, quoting Euphrosyne.

'I don't understand that,' said Jenny flatly.

'It means you have to lump it!' her sister told her, appropriating the balls briskly.

The men folk were much refreshed after their naps, and over tea Lovell spoke of the Boxing Day meet which was always held in the square of the local market town.

'Shall we go?' he asked.

'Yes, yes!' chorused the children. 'All in one car! All squashed up and cosy. And take our presents so we can play while we wait!'

Lovell looked at Miriam. She thought quickly. Certainly lunch would be cold turkey, and that presented no difficulties, but she longed to attack some of the more urgent cleaning that had obviously been neglected since Eileen's departure. She did not want Lovell to see her scrubbing his kitchen floor, but that was what she had planned to do if she could manage it unobserved. Then there was the gammon to cook, and a vast amount of necessary sweeping and dusting to do. To have two hours alone would suit her plans perfectly.

'I think I'll stay here if you don't mind,' she replied. 'There are several things to do, and I really ought to ring Joan. I shall probably catch her in the morning.'

'Of course, of course,' said Lovell. He spoke sympathetically. To his eyes, the girl looked absolutely exhausted and he felt horribly guilty. She worked hard at the office, had undertaken a long journey, and was coping superbly with his family. Obviously, it would do her good to have a brief time on her own.

'I'll take the brood off soon after ten,' he promised. 'The meet is at eleven, and we'll be back before one o'clock.'

'Marvellous!' said Miriam, with relief.

The rest of the day passed quietly. Lovell went to the hospital to see Eileen, and the children, tired after all the excitement, were docile enough to go to bed early.

Miriam put the gammon to boil, averted her eyes from the state of the kitchen floor, and fell, bone-weary, into an armchair.

A vision of Holly Lodge as it would be in the New Year, if she ever returned to her ministrations there, floated before her. Quiet, warm, clean – a haven of solitude and silence – it hung before her mind's eye as beautiful as a jewel.

She sighed, and slept.

CHAPTER NINE

It was overcast when Miriam awoke next morning. From her bedroom window she looked out across the flat countryside towards the sea, some twenty miles away.

Inky-dark clouds were moving in slowly, dwarfing the trees and farmsteads with menacing stature. Already, a boisterous wind was blowing, and Miriam predicted storms before long. She only hoped that the rain would hold off long enough for the family to enjoy the Meet.

They all drove off in high spirits, and Miriam returned from waving goodbye to tackle the worst of the mess.

She tidied the larder, ruthlessly throwing away the flotsam and jetsam of the past week, stale bread, ancient scraps of cheese, decaying and unidentifiable morsels on saucers, withered apples and the like. The birds descended in a flock, sea-gulls among the more usual visitors, and snapped up this bounty.

She scrubbed the sink and draining boards, thankful that, with all its drawbacks, the vicarage was blessed with plenty of hot water.

There was something rather satisfying, she found, in scrubbing the tiles of the kitchen floor. The clean sweet-smelling wetness, which grew as she retreated backwards from it on her knees, delighted her, and although she doubted if anyone would ever notice the result of her labours, she was content with her small reward of a job well done.

That finished, she mounted the steep stairs, manhandling the vacuum sweeper and dusters, and set about the bedrooms. The chaos of the girls' room was daunting, and the fact that the dirty linen basket was overflowing was another reminder of work ahead. Really, thought Miriam, dusting vigorously, I should never have made a wife and mother! Looking after Barney from nine till five is more than enough for me!

By twelve-thirty the house looked reasonably tidy, and she skinned the gammon, gave up a fruitless search for bread crumbs with which to adorn it, and set the table. It was while she was doing this that she heard the car return, and voices in the hall.

She emerged from the kitchen to find that Lovell was accompanied by another man.

Who could this stranger be? She looked again, and hurried forward smiling.

'Why, Martin, how lovely to see you again!'

'Brought him back from the Meet for a drink,' said Lovell beaming. 'It must be nearly a year since we met.'

'And more like ten since I saw Miriam,' said Martin. 'And as elegant as ever.'

They moved into the sitting-room, the children following.

'You run and play in the garden for a few minutes,' directed Lovell.

'But we're hungry!'

'When is lunch ready?'

'Can't we have a drink too?'

The protests came thick and fast.

'Have an apple each,' suggested Miriam diplomatically, 'and go and practise two-ball.'

This solution pleased all, and the adults were left to sip their sherry in peace.

It appeared that Martin Farrar's farm lay some twelve miles on the other side of the market town.

'Corn mainly, and sugar beet,' he told Miriam, 'though I keep a few head of cattle. I'm hoping to have pigs some day too. But tell me your news. Where do you live now?'

Miriam told him about the job in Caxley, and her new home at Holly Lodge. She found herself rattling away – Martin had always been a good listener, she remembered – and was about to enlarge on her interrupted decorating of the sitting-room when she remembered Lovell's feelings, and checked herself.

'I stopped in Cambridge, on the journey up,' she said instead, and that opened the way to a flood of happy reminiscences.

'You'll stay to lunch, won't you?' said Lovell. He turned to Miriam anxiously. 'Is it all right? It's cold turkey, I believe?'

'Quite right. And gammon too. And it will be lovely if you can stop.'

'I'd love to,' said Martin.

Miriam retired to the kitchen to finish her preparations. She was slightly puzzled. What about Martin's wife? Would she be waiting lunch for him? No mention had been made of her. Perhaps she was away. But, at Christmas time? Had they parted?

Perplexed, she assembled pickles and an un-opened giant-size packet of potato crisps. She put in the oven the batch of mince pies she had made earlier, and hoped that the cheese board would provide for any empty corners left by the lunch she had prepared.

The children ate hungrily, their appetites whetted by the fresh air. As they ate, the first of the raindrops spattered against the window, and the wind began to roar more loudly.

'We're in for it, I'm afraid,' said Martin. 'The glass was going back this morning. As long as we don't get snow, I don't mind.'

'Do you remember the winter of 1962 and 1963?' asked Lovell. 'My parents were marooned in the vicarage for four weeks, with eight-foot drifts cutting them off. Thank God, my mother always did a lot of bottling and preserving. Father said he hoped never to face another bottled gooseberry in his lifetime!'

'We were just married,' said Martin, 'and had mis-judged the fuel amounts. Binnie walked about clutching a hot-water bottle all day. It taught us to stock up properly another time.'

'I was in London,' said Miriam, 'a bitter waste of brown slush everywhere. Town snow is so much worse than country snow.'

After lunch, the little girls elected to paint at the kitchen table and Miriam left them to enjoy the new paints and painting books while she put Robin to bed, and Lovell made coffee.

The rain now lashed the house, and Miriam stuffed the towel again into the vulnerable landing window before going downstairs to the fireside.

Martin was helping himself to Lovell's brew and surveying the weather.

'I ought to be getting back pretty soon. I'm the cattle man this afternoon, and it's going to get dark early today.'

They sat at peace, enjoying the warmth of the fire and their coffee.

Miriam looked at Martin as he gazed somnolently at the blazing logs. He had worn well. His hair was thick, his face tanned with his outdoor life, and he was as lean as he had always been. And yet, there was an air of unhappiness about him. Perhaps he felt the same about herself. Perhaps it was simply the passing of the years, the change from the effervescence of youth to the sobriety of middle-age.

Middle-age! It was a shock to realize that she was half-way to her three-score years and ten. Martin must be nearing forty.

He put his cup down in the hearth with a clatter, and stretched luxuriously.

'Oh, if I could only stay by this fire! Instead, I must go back and bash swedes.'

'Do you really bash swedes?' asked Miriam.

'Not today,' said Martin, with a laugh. 'Just feed the cattle with something less demanding.'

He held out his hand.

'Thank you for giving me lunch, and for your company. I come your way about twice a year. Perhaps I may call in, now I know where you live?'

'I shall look forward to it.'

'Well, it may be in a few weeks' time. There's a cattle dealer in Wales I want to see.'

He made his farewells, and they watched him race through the rain to his Land-Rover. The rain was now torrential, and the branches clashed overhead in the force of the gale, but Martin's grin was cheerful as he waved goodbye.

'Nice to see him again,' said Lovell as they shut the door against the weather. 'We live so near really, and were such close friends in the old days, it seems absurd to lose touch as we have done.'

The fireside was doubly snug after their brush with the weather outside. Peace reigned in the kitchen, and Robin slept aloft. Miriam and Lovell resumed their seats with relief.

She lay back, musing about the encounter. It was good to see Martin again. Their early flirtation had been a happy one, and it was comforting to see, once again, the unfeigned affection and admiration in his looks. She hoped she would see him again when he travelled to Wales next.

'What is Martin's wife like?' she asked.

'Martin's wife?' Lovell looked startled.

'Binnie, he called her,' said Miriam.

Lovell shook his head sadly.

'Poor Binnie! I should have remembered that you knew nothing about it. She died two years ago – quite that, longer perhaps. I can't quite remember.'

'How ghastly for Martin! What was it?'

'One of those incredibly stupid accidents that strain one's religious beliefs sorely. She was bathing within a few yards of the shore, when a freak wave carried her out to sea, and a sort of whirlpool sucked her under. There were treacherous currents there always, we heard later.'

'Was Martin there?'

'He had gone to fetch towels from the car, and returned

to find the rescue operation going on. The ghastly thing was that the body wasn't washed up until the next tide.'

'Poor Martin! And no children?'

'There was one on the way, which made it worse, of course. I heard Martin was in an appalling state of shock for months. His old mother was a tower of strength, and went to live at the farm with him.'

'I remember her,' replied Miriam, recalling the ramrod figure of Mrs Farrar, her white hair and her deep voice. 'Dreadful for her too.'

'Anyway,' said Lovell, 'he seems to have recovered, and let's hope he may find someone else one day.'

'That's Robin,' exclaimed Miriam, at the sound of a distant wailing.

And she went to resume her duties.

She travelled alone to see Eileen that evening, Lovell volunteering to see his family into bed.

As she drove through the roaring night, buffeted by a fierce north-easter, she suddenly remembered that she had still forgotten to telephone Joan. Martin's arrival had put it out of her head.

Lovell's account of Martin's tragedy had moved her deeply. Why did these things have to happen? Lovell's comment about the strain on one's religious beliefs, in the face of such senseless horror, was understandable. If he, so secure and ardent in his faith, could feel thus, how easy it was to forgive weaker souls who turned against their religion in such circumstances. Martin appeared to have weathered his own storm remarkably well. Possibly, the fact that his work must go on in rain or shine had helped him through the worst. She was glad she knew about it, if she were to see him in the future. When she had said that she would look forward to seeing him again, she had spoken from her heart.

Eileen was wearing the new black nightgown, and looked prettier than ever. She was in good spirits.

'I ought to know very soon if I'm coming home next week,' she told Miriam. 'How I long for it! Tell me, how are you managing?'

Miriam told her the scraps of news, how helpful the children had been, how she had introduced them to two-ball, how beautiful the church had looked decked for Christmas and, finally, how Lovell had brought Martin to lunch.

Eileen's face lit up.

'I'm so glad! We feel so terribly sorry for him, and we wish we saw more of him. He ought to marry again. He's such a dear.'

She looked at Miriam with such an openly speculative eye that it was impossible not to laugh. Eileen laughed too, with such infectious gaiety that the woman in the next bed said: 'She's as good as a tonic is Mrs Quinn!'

And it was then that Miriam suddenly realized that here was a new neighbour. Mrs White, of the grey sad countenance, had gone, it seemed, to a colder bed under the Norfolk sky.

'I'm not really match-making,' said Eileen lightly.

'I should hope not,' replied Miriam. 'Tell me, how did Christmas Day go in here?'

Eileen was willing to be deflected from the subject of Martin, much to Miriam's relief, and launched into a spirited account of the chief surgeon's prowess in turkey-carving, the morning carols, and the visit of the Mayor and his retinue.

Miriam stayed later than she intended, revelling in Eileen's racy descriptions, and the undoubted fact that she seemed stronger and more relaxed after her few days in hospital.

'You'll have Annie back on Monday,' said Eileen, as they said goodbye. 'And with any luck, I'll be home very soon after.'

'We'll have a grand celebration,' promised Miriam, fastening her coat, before leaving the warmth of the ward to face the gales outside.

CHAPTER TEN

The weekend passed remarkably peacefully. Miriam felt more confident now that she was becoming accustomed to the routine of the household. One great blessing was that all the family seemed to eat most of the things she put before them, although turkey in a mild cheese sauce was greeted by Jenny with the remark that she 'didn't like white gravy'. However, her helping vanished, assisted, no doubt, by Hazel's offer to eat her share.

The craze for two-ball persisted, and the two little girls spent any rain-free periods – which were few – bouncing and catching the balls against the wall of the kitchen garden, twirling and clapping as Miriam had shown them.

It seemed a good idea to drive into the market town on Saturday morning, in the hope that a toy shop would be open. They were lucky enough to find a sports shop doing a brisk trade with two girls buying ski-ing equipment and a scoutmaster buying camping stoves. A basket of rubber balls, red, blue, yellow and green, drew Hazel and Jenny like a magnet, and they ended by selecting two red and two green.

'I think you should have three each,' said Miriam. 'You ought to have a spare in case one gets lost.'

'But can you afford it?' asked Hazel anxiously. 'After Christmas too?'

'I think so,' said Miriam.

'But you haven't got a husband to give you any money like Mummy,' protested Jenny. 'Are you sure?'

'I go to work, you know, so I earn some money.'

'A lot? A pound a week?'

'A little more than that,' admitted Miriam.

The girls sighed with relief.

'Then you're quite rich, aren't you?' smiled Hazel.

'Well then, thank you very much,' said Jenny, choosing a yellow one for her spare ball. 'You are kind, as well as rich.'

The baker's shop was open next door, and Miriam bought fresh currant buns for tea, and a veal and ham pie as a change from the turkey.

'You must be *really* rich,' observed Hazel, as they climbed into the car with their purchases, 'if you can buy a great big pie like that. Mummy always makes ours, because she says they are so dear in the shops.'

'Well, this is a treat,' explained Miriam. And a time and energy saver for a struggling aunt, she added to herself.

She found time to ring Joan, who sounded busy and happy.

'Roger goes tomorrow. A friend is picking him up and they are flying to Switzerland at six o'clock. Plenty of snow there, they say.'

'None at Fairacre, I hope?'

'Not yet, but it's cold enough.'

They exchanged news. Barbara and the family were off on the Monday. And when could Joan hope to see Miriam?

'With luck, during next week,' said Miriam. 'It depends if Eileen is allowed home, and how strong she feels.'

'Well, Holly Lodge is waiting for you,' said Joan. 'So come as soon as you can.'

'I can promise that,' Miriam assured her.

The gales continued, rising to their height on Sunday night. There were tales of fishing-boats smashed at their moorings, and of large ships riding out the storm within sight of the Norfolk coast. At places the sea had flooded the marshland, and great damage was reported from the seaside towns on the Norfolk and Suffolk coasts. Men spent the weekend filling sandbags to block the gaps in the sea wall where the violence of the high tide had breached it.

At the vicarage, some tiles were blown from the roof and an ancient apple tree was toppled, its roots exposed to the children's horrified gaze, and its branches enmeshing a chicken house which was mercifully empty.

For the first time, Miriam saw the children frightened that night. The house shuddered in the onslaught, and the banshee wailings, which Miriam had thought belonged to the kitchen only, were increased to envelop the upstairs corridors.

Miriam left a night-light burning in a saucer of water to comfort the little girls. The tall shadows, made by the brave little light, took her back in an instant to her own childhood in just such a bleak vicarage, and she kissed the little girls with extra warmth and sympathy.

The nine o'clock news was devoted largely to the havoc caused by the storm, related with the usual zest with which the imparting of bad news is passed on. Shades of Mrs Pringle, thought Miriam, watching a woman smugly explaining how she had found her neighbour pinned beneath her own coal-shed and describing, with relish, the extent of her injuries.

'That's enough of that!' said Lovell, switching it off. 'If I know anything about it, it will have blown itself out within twenty-four hours.'

It was at twelve the next day that the telephone rang, and it was Eileen on the line, sounding highly jubilant.

'It looks as though I can come home tomorrow. Isn't it wonderful? Can Lovell fetch me in the afternoon? The doctor wants to see me in the morning, and it's really simpler if I have lunch here.'

'Marvellous!' cried Miriam. 'Let me call Lovell. He's in the garden, sawing the apple tree into logs.'

'Any damage?'

'Very little,' Miriam told her, 'and the wind is dying down nicely.'

'Look out for floods by the river,' warned Eileen. 'The papers haven't arrived yet, and they say a lot of people have had to leave their houses in the low-lying part of the town. Poor things! Can you imagine anything worse than finding your carpets floating downstairs?'

'Yes. Floating upstairs. Here's Lovell now,' called Miriam, handing over the telephone to her wind-blown brother.

She could hear the excitement in his voice as she returned to the mound of washing which she was tackling. With any luck, she thought, it would be dry and ironed before the mistress of the house returned. And tomorrow morning, she must go foraging for food again.

That afternoon, when she and the children returned from a windy walk, they found Annie on the doorstep.

The children rushed to greet her. Robin put his arms up round her waist and kissed the fourth button of her raincoat rapturously.

'How lovely to see you,' cried Miriam. 'Come in, and tell me what you usually do.'

'Well,' said Annie, 'I help to get tea, and then I bath Robin, and then I do anything Mrs Quinn wants – ironing usually, or a bit of mending, and then I help put Jenny and Hazel to bed and then I go home.'

She was a thick-set cheerful girl with long straight hair tied in a pony-tail and the brightest dark eyes which Miriam had ever seen.

'That sounds wonderful,' said Miriam. 'Let's get tea together now, and I'll start the ironing while you put Robin to bed later on.'

'And my mum said, as it's school holidays and Mrs Quinn's been took bad, I can come most of the day, just when it helps. I could do shopping at that, and take the children out for their walk. Just what's best.'

'You are an angel,' said Miriam fervently. 'I'll speak to Mr Quinn when he comes in, and we'll arrange something.'

Tea was taken at the kitchen table, and Miriam could see how competent and calm the young girl was with her charges, and how much they adored her. It was a noisy meal, with constant interruptions to fetch new toys to be admired. No doubt about it, thought Miriam, Annie was a treasure.

Miriam heard Lovell come in, and hurried into the sitting-room to tell him the good news.

'God bless Annie!' he said sincerely. 'For this week anyway, it would seem perfect if she came, say, at eleven and had coffee with us, and stayed the rest of the day, up till the children's bedtime, if her mother is agreeable.'

'Go and have a word with her,' suggested Miriam.

And so, to everyone's relief and joy, matters were arranged.

Annie's addition to the household was certainly a blessing, as Miriam soon discovered. By the time she arrived on Tuesday morning, Miriam had put Eileen and Lovell's bedroom to rights, had changed sheets, put out fresh soap and towels, and even found a few sprigs of yellow winter jasmine to put in a little vase by Eileen's bed.

Annie departed towards the village, after her coffee, with a long shopping list, three baskets and the children. Copper decided to accompany them too, and for the first time Miriam found herself the only living thing in the house; Lovell was out visiting sick parishioners.

It was bliss to have the kitchen to herself, and to be able to follow a train of thought without urgent infant demands for attention. She prepared lunch, and even made a large batch of shortbread which, with any luck, could be stored in a tin for future use when she herself had gone back to Fairacre.

She had purposely made no firm plans for her return. It all depended on Eileen, but secretly she longed to get back within the next few days to finish her sitting-room and to be ready for the office on the following Monday.

Her meditations were soon interrupted by the return of Annie and her charges, and the necessity of storing away shopping and setting the table for lunch.

'Why can't we go with Daddy to fetch Mummy?' complained Hazel.

'Because it will be much nicer to get things ready for her here,' said Miriam firmly. 'You can put a hot bottle in her bed in case she feels tired, and Jenny can get the tea-tray ready.'

They looked doubtful about these arrangements but fell in with the plans without argument. On such a joyous occasion, fighting seemed out of place.

As if to add to the general air of festivity, the sun had come out, and the wind was less violent, although strong enough to send great galleons of white cloud scudding across the blue sky. On the wide Norfolk fields below, the clouds chased each other across hedges and ditches, so that the countryside was alternately lit with golden sunshine and deepest shadow. The change in the weather brought a refreshment of spirit, and when at last Lovell's car drew up at the front door, and Eileen emerged with arms outstretched, the family burst from the front door with cries of excitement.

'Do you want to go to bed?' demanded Hazel, when their mother was at last sitting by the fire.

'Heavens, no!' cried Eileen. 'Why?'

'Because I've put in a bottle for you.'

'That's very kind, but it will do beautifully for later on.'

'Have some tea,' urged Jenny, anxious to display her preparations.

'Not at three, darling,' said her mother. 'Just let me sit and look at you all and the house. It's so marvellous to be back. And how *clean* everything looks!'

Miriam was amused to find herself as gratified with this last compliment as she was when Barney gave her a rare pat on the back for some meticulously arranged

conference, or for some particularly diplomatic handling of a difficult client.

It was good to see the family united again, and to see too how much Annie was included in the general reunion. Eileen was genuinely touched at the girl's offer of help while she was on holiday, and when at last the young people went off in her charge, Eileen spoke of her to Miriam.

'She's absolutely splendid with children. We hope she'll be able to take up nursery training. It's what she wants to do, and Lovell and I are going to do all we can to persuade her mother to let her. She's about the most unselfish person I ever met – next to you, I should say.'

'Not me!' protested Miriam. 'I am *horribly* selfish. All I think about is my own affairs.'

'Then the virtue is all the greater when you put them aside so readily to come to our aid,' said Eileen firmly.

Later that evening when the children were abed and Annie had departed, the three sat by the fire in amicable drowsiness.

'Are you sure you wouldn't sooner be in bed?' asked Miriam.

'No, it's bliss to be here, and honestly I feel better, if anything, than when I went in. The diet's helped a lot, and all I need now is a little exercise to get my legs less wobbly.'

'You look more relaxed,' agreed Lovell, 'but I shouldn't venture out for a day or two. After that hot-house of a hospital you'll find the vicarage garden pretty chilly.'

'Pottering round the house will suit me,' said Eileen. 'And I hope Miriam will stay on now for a holiday instead of being a hard-working housekeeper, and let me look after her, for a change.'

'I shall stay as long as I'm needed,' said Miriam, 'but let's see how you feel tomorrow morning before we make plans. I've thoroughly enjoyed myself here. It's been a break—'

'*But*,' broke in Eileen, 'you have your own affairs to see to, and we've trespassed on your precious free time already. Honestly, my darling Miriam, I am perfectly recovered, and I think next week's check-up will be the last that's needed, so if you want to go ahead with your own plans, *please* feel free.'

'Well,' said Miriam, weakening in the face of this reasoning, 'let's decide tomorrow morning. If all is well, perhaps I could go on Thursday. Now that Annie's here—'

'Even if Annie weren't here, we could manage, I feel sure. Lovell can be here pretty well non-stop until Sunday, and the girls are quite big enough to help now.'

At that moment the telephone rang and Lovell went to answer it. He returned to say:

'It's for you, Miriam. It's Martin on the telephone.'

'Look, Miriam,' said Martin, 'this Welsh trip has cropped up sooner than I thought. The dealer has some good cattle at the moment, and I propose going down on Saturday and coming back on Sunday. Can we meet?'

Miriam thought quickly.

'What about Sunday lunch with me? Something pretty simple, as I'm in the throes of decorating and the paint may still be wet, but—'

'No, no. I insist on taking you out to lunch. But Sunday will be fine for me. Do you know somewhere?'

'I'll book a table in Caxley,' said Miriam. 'Shall we say twelve-thirty at "The Bull"? It's just off the Market Square.'

'Lovely!' said Martin. 'Now we've found each other again, it will be good to catch up with old times.'

'Yes, indeed,' said Miriam politely. But she wished he had said: 'Now we've *met* each other again' instead of '*found each other*' which sounded uncomfortably intimate to one of her temperament.

'Martin's coming my way next weekend,' she said, returning to the fireside. 'And taking me out to lunch.'

'Well, he hasn't lost much time,' said Lovell, with a satisfaction which his sister found distasteful in the circumstances. But she forbore to retort.

*

Next morning, to her surprise, she found that Eileen was in the kitchen before her, and was busy frying bacon and eggs for the family.

She smiled at Miriam's astonishment.

'This is just to show you how fit I am. I feel a positive fraud being treated as an invalid.'

'How did you sleep?'

'Like a top. Woke up an hour ago feeling I could mow the lawn, walk to Norwich, and eat a couple of horses.'

'Wonderful! You've certainly recovered.'

She began to cut bread ready to toast. It was good to see Eileen in command again.

'So, Miriam dear, don't linger here on our behalf if you really want to get back. I couldn't help overhearing your remark to Martin that you were in the midst of decorating. You are an absolute marvel to have dropped everything – paint brushes included – to come all this way.'

She put down the fork with which she was turning the bacon and came to put her arms around Miriam.

'This isn't speeding the parting guest. I'd like you to stay, you know, but if you can't now, then come very soon for a real holiday. But if you'd feel happier about getting back, please believe me when I say we can really manage now, and will *never* forget your kindness when we were in trouble.'

Miriam hugged her affectionately.

'If you're quite sure, then I might even push off later this morning. The weather seems more settled, and if Annie turns up as usual, I'd feel quite happy about leaving you with that stout support.'

And so it fell out that at half past eleven, with her case in the car, sandwiches cut by Eileen, a flask filled by Annie, and a posy of mixed winter flowers collected by the children, Miriam was ready to start on her long journey.

All the family, including Annie, were on the doorstep to wave goodbye. Their embraces had been unusually warm and loving, and Miriam was astonished to realize how sad she felt at parting. To think that just over a week ago she had arrived in a mood of stern duty! Now it was as much as she could do to keep back the tears as she drove away.

'Don't forget you're coming at Easter!' shouted Hazel.

'Before if you can!' added Eileen.

'A thousand thanks!' called Lovell. 'I shall be writing.'

She hooted all the way down the drive in reply to their valedictions, and had to fumble for a handkerchief when she was safely out of their sight.

The floods were out between St Neots and Bedford, and traffic was diverted round narrow lanes bordering water-logged fields. At Newport Pagnell there were more floods, but the sky was clear and the wind had dropped to a gentle breeze, and Miriam pushed on steadily.

There was plenty of time now for uninterrupted thought. A lot of good had come from this week's visit. She had learnt to know Eileen better and to appreciate the strength of character that lay behind the babyish good looks. She remembered her gaiety and courage in the face of death at the hospital, her honest gratitude for help given. Now she began to see why Lovell loved her so much. It made her own feelings towards her brother much more comfortable. If Lovell were happy, then she too was happy. It was as simple as that.

And how much greater now was her bond with the children! They were all of them – Lovell, Eileen and she herself – much closer because of this adversity. She felt better for having gone. It had jolted her out of her own selfish rut, and a good thing too, she told herself.

'*Cast your bread upon the waters!*' she remembered. Well, she had certainly received a bountiful return.

It was dark when she arrived at Holly Lodge, and Joan was out. Probably having a New Year's Eve drink with

friends in Fairacre, thought Miriam, suddenly remembering the date.

She put away the car, and carried her things indoors. The pleasant smell of new paint greeted her. She breathed it in with rapture.

Here she was at last! At home, and alone, ready for all that might befall in the New Year.

What would it hold for her? She remembered Martin, and was warmed by the thought of his friendship which might grow – who knew? – into something dearer.

Well, it was nice to be wanted, Lovell and his family had proved that. But not for always, thought Miriam, looking for a vase for her Norfolk nosegay. She was glad to have met Martin again, glad to know she would see him soon, and glad to know that the bond with her family was more closely knit.

But this was where she was happiest. For her, spinster-hood was truly blessed. She walked into her empty sitting-room and closed the door behind her, the better to relish that sweet solitude which to her was the breath of life.

A vision of the vicarage rose before her – the paper chains, the expanding fans and bells, the tinsel, the mistletoe, the holly.

Here there was no holly for Miss Quinn, but she felt a glow as warm as its red berries at the joy of being home, a joy which, she knew, would remain ever green in the years which lay ahead.

Christmas at Fairacre School

Miss Read is the head teacher at the small school in the downland village of Fairacre, and she is the narrator in the many books about Fairacre. Here she describes the scene at the end of term as the school prepares to break up for the Christmas holidays.

Preparations for Christmas are now in full swing. For weeks past, the shops in Caxley have been a blaze of coloured lights and decorated with Father Christmases, decked trees, silver balls and all the other paraphernalia. Even our grocer's shop in Fairacre has cotton-wool snow, hanging on threads, down the window, and this, together with the crib already set up in the church, all add to the children's enchantment.

It has turned bitterly cold, with a cruel east wind which has scattered the last of the leaves and ruffles the feathers of the birds who sit among the bare branches. The tortoise stoves are kept roaring away, but nothing can cure the fiendish draught from the skylight above my desk, and the one from the door, where generations of feet have worn the lintel into a hollow.

Yesterday afternoon the whole school was busy making Christmas decorations and Christmas cards. There is nothing that children like more than making brightly-coloured paper chains, and their tongues wagged happily as the paste brushes were plied, and yet another glowing link was added to the festoons that lay heaped on the floor. All this glory grows so deliciously quickly and the knowledge that, very soon, it will be swinging aloft above their heads among the pitch-pine rafters – an enchanting token of all the joys that Christmas holds in store – makes them work with more than usual energy.

In Miss Jackson's room the din was terrific, so excited were the chain-makers. The only quiet group here was the one which was composed of about eight small children who had elected to crayon Christmas cards instead. Among them was the little Pratt boy. I stopped to admire his effort. His picture was of a large and dropsical robin, with the fiercest of red breasts and very small and inadequate legs, as there was only a quarter of an inch of space left at the bottom for these highly necessary appendages. His face was solemn with the absorption of the true artist.

'It's for Miss Bunce,' he told me. 'You knows – the one at Barrisford what took me to the hostipple to have my eye done. She writes to me ever so often, and sometimes sends me sweets. D'you reckon she'll like it?'

He held up his masterpiece and surveyed it anxiously at arm's length.

I told him truthfully that I was sure she would like it very much, and that all sensible people liked robins on Christmas cards. With a sigh of infinite satisfaction he replaced it on the desk, and prepared to face the horrid intricacies of writing 'HAPPY CHRISTMAS' inside.

By right and ancient custom at Fairacre School the last afternoon of the Christmas term is given up to a tea-party.

The partition had been pushed back so that the two classrooms were thrown into one, but even so the school was crowded – with children, parents and friends. Mrs Finch-Edwards was there, showing her baby daughter Althea to Miss Clare. Miss Jackson, who had dressed the Christmas tree alone, was receiving congratulations upon its glittering beauty from Miss Partridge. Mr Robert's hearty laugh rustled the paper-chains so near his head, and the vicar beamed upon us all, until Mrs Pringle gave him the school cutting-out scissors and reminded him of his responsibilities. For it was he who would cut the dangling presents from the tree before the party ended.

Mrs Coggs and Mrs Waites had walked up together from Tyler's Row, and now sat, side by side, watching their sons engulf sardine sandwiches, iced biscuits, sponge cake, jam tarts and sausage rolls, all washed down with frequent draughts of fizzy lemonade through a gurgling straw. Mr Willet, at one end of the room, had the job of taking the metal tops off the bottles, and with bent back, and purple, sweating face, had been hard put to it to keep pace with the demand.

It was a cheerful scene. The paper-chains and lanterns

swung from the rafters, the tortoise stoves, especially brilliant today from Mrs Pringle's ministrations, roared merrily, and the glittering tree dominated the room.

The children, flushed with food, heat and excitement, chattered like starlings, and around them the warm, country voices of their elders exchanged news and gossip.

After tea, the old well-loved games were played, 'Oranges and Lemons' with Miss Clare at the piano, and Mr and Mrs Partridge making the arch, 'Poor Jenny sits a-weeping', 'The Farmer's in his Den', 'Nuts and May' and 'Hunt the Thimble'. We always have this one last of all so that we can regain our breath. The children nearly burst with suppressed excitement as the seeker wandered bewildered about the room, and on this occasion the roars of 'Cold, cold!' or 'Warmer, warmer!' and the wild yielding of 'Hot, hot! You're *real* hot!' nearly raised the pitch-pine roof.

The presents were cut from the tree, and the afternoon finished with carols, old and young singing together lustily and with sincerity. Within those familiar walls, feuds and old hurts forgotten, for an hour or two at least, Fairacre had been united in joy and true goodwill.

It was dark when the party ended. Farewells and Christmas greetings had been exchanged under the night sky, and the schoolroom was dishevelled but quiet. The Christmas tree, denuded of its parcels and awaiting the removal of its bright baubles on the morrow, still had place of honour in the centre of the floor.

Joseph Coggs' dark eyes had been fixed so longingly on the star at its summit that Miss Clare had unfastened it and given it into his keeping when the rest of the children had been safely out of the way.

The voices and footsteps had died away long ago by the time I was ready to lock up and go across to my peaceful house. Some of the bigger children were coming in the morning to help me clear up the aftermath of our Christmas revels, before Mrs Pringle started her holiday scrubbing.

The great Gothic door swung to with a clang, and I turned the key. The night was still and frosty. From the distant downs came the faint bleating of Mr Roberts' sheep, and the lowing of the bull in a nearby field. Suddenly a cascade of sound showered from St Patrick's spire. The bell-ringers were practising their Christmas peal. After that first mad jangle the bells fell sweetly into place, steadily, rhythmically, joyfully calling their message across the clustered roofs and the plumes of smoke from Fairacre's hearths, to the grey, bare glory of the downs that shelter us.

I turned to go home, and to my amazement, noticed a child standing by the school gate.

It was Joseph Coggs. High above his head he held his tinsel star, squinting at it lovingly as he compared it with those which winked in their thousands from above St Patrick's spire.

We stood looking at it together, and it was some time before he spoke, raising his voice against the clamour of the bells.

'Good, ain't it?' he said, with the utmost satisfaction.

'Very good!' I agreed.

The Christmas Mouse

*To Elizabeth Ann Green
who started this story*

CHAPTER ONE

The rain began at noon.

At first it fell lightly, making little noise. Only the darkening of the thatched roofs, and the sheen on the damp flagstones made people aware of the rain. It was dismissed as 'only a mizzle'. Certainly it did not warrant bringing in the tea towels from the line. Midday meals were taken in the confident belief that the shower would soon blow over. Why, the weathermen had predicted a calm spell, hadn't they, only that morning?

But by two o'clock it was apparent that something was radically wrong with the weather forecast. The wind had swung round to the northwest, and the drizzle had turned to a downpour. It hissed among the dripping trees,

pattered upon the cabbages in cottage gardens and drummed the bare soil with pock marks.

Mrs Berry, at her kitchen window, watched the clouds of rain drifting across the fields, obscuring the distant wood and veiling the whole countryside. A vicious gust of wind flung a spatter of raindrops against the pane with so much force that it might have been a handful of gravel hurled in the old lady's face. She did not flinch, but instead raised her voice against the mounting fury of the storm.

'What a day,' said Mrs Berry, 'for Christmas Eve!'

Behind her, kneeling on the rush matting, her daughter Mary was busy buttoning her two little girls into their mackintoshes.

'Hold still,' she said impatiently, 'hold still, do! We'll never catch the bus at this rate.'

They were fidgeting with excitement. Their cheeks were flushed, their eyes sparkling. It was as much as they could do to lift their chins for their mother to fasten the stiff top buttons of their new red mackintoshes. But the reminder that the bus might go without them checked their excitement. Only two afternoon buses a week ran past the cottage, one on market day, and one on Saturday. To miss it meant missing the last-minute shopping expedition for the really important Christmas presents – those for their mother and grandmother. The idea of being deprived of this joy brought the little girls to partial submission.

Mary, her fingers busy with the buttons, was thinking of more mundane shopping – Brussels sprouts, some salad, a little pot of cranberry jelly for the turkey, a few more oranges if they were not too expensive, a lemon or two. And a potted plant for Mum. A cyclamen perhaps? Or a heather, if the cyclamen proved to be beyond her purse. It was mean the way these florists put up the prices so cruelly at Christmas. But there, she told herself, scrambling to her feet, the poor souls had to live the same as she did, she supposed, and with everything costing so much they would have to look after themselves like anyone else.

'You wait here quietly with Gran for a minute,' she adjured the pair, 'while I run and get my coat on, and fetch the baskets. Got your money and your hankies? Don't want no sniffing on the bus now!'

She whisked upstairs and the children could hear her hurrying to and fro above the beamed ceiling of the kitchen.

Old Mrs Berry was opening her brown leather purse. There were not many coins in it, and no notes, but she took out two silver fivepenny pieces.

'To go towards your shopping,' said the old lady. 'Hold out your hands.'

Two small hands, encased in woollen gloves knitted by Mrs Berry herself, were eagerly outstretched.

'Jane first,' said Mrs Berry, putting the coin into the older girl's hand. 'And now Frances.'

'Thank you, Gran, thank you,' they chorused, throwing their arms round her comfortable bulk, pressing wet kisses upon her.

'No need to tell your mum,' said Mrs Berry. 'It's a little secret between us three. Here she comes.'

The three hurried to the cottage door. The rain was coming down in sheets, and Mary struggled with an umbrella on the threshold.

'Dratted thing' – she puffed – 'but can't do without it today. I'll wager I forget it in some shop, but there it is. Come on now, you girls. Keep close to me, and run for it!'

Mrs Berry watched them vanish into the swirling rain. Then she shut the door upon the weather, and returned to the peaceful kitchen.

She put her wrinkled hand upon the teapot. Good, it was still hot. She would have another cup before she washed up.

Sitting in the wooden armchair that had been her husband's, Mrs Berry surveyed the kitchen with pleasure. It had been decorated a few years before and young Bertie, Mary's husband, had made a good job of it. The walls were white, the curtains cherry-red cotton, and the tiles round the sink were blue and white. Bertie, who had set them so neatly, said they came from a fireplace over in Oxfordshire and were from Holland originally. The builder, a friend of his, was about to throw them out but Bertie had rescued them.

A clever boy with his hands, thought Mrs Berry, stirring her tea, though she could never understand what poor Mary saw in him, with that sandy hair and those white eyelashes. Still, it did no good to think ill of the dead, and he had made a good husband and father for the few short years he and Mary had been married. This would be the third Christmas without him – a sad time for Mary, poor soul.

Mrs Berry had once wondered if this youngest daughter of hers would ever marry. The two older girls were barely twenty when they wed. One was a farmer's wife near Taunton. The other had married an American, and Mrs Berry had only seen her twice since.

Mary, the prettiest of the three girls, had never been one for the boys. After she left school, she worked in the village post office at Springbourne, cycling to work in all weather and seeming content to read and knit or tend the garden when she returned at night.

Mrs Berry was glad of her daughter's company. She had been widowed in 1953, after over thirty years of tranquil marriage to dear Stanley. He had been a stone-mason, attached to an old-established firm in Caxley, and he too cycled daily to work, his tools strapped securely on the carrier with his midday sandwiches. On a day as wild and wet as this Christmas Eve, he had arrived home soaked through. That night he tossed in a fever, muttering in delirium, and within a week he was dead – the victim of a particularly virulent form of influenza.

In the weeks of shock and mourning that followed, Mary was a tower of strength to her mother. Once the funeral was over, and replies had been sent to all the friends and relatives who had written in sympathy, the two women took stock of their situation. Thank God, the cottage was her own, Mrs Berry said. It had taken the savings of a lifetime to buy when it came on the market, but now they had a roof over their heads and no weekly rent to find. There was a tiny pension from Stanley's firm, a few pounds in the post office savings bank, and Mary's weekly wage. Two mornings of housework every week at the Manor Farm brought in a few more shillings for Mrs Berry. And the farmer's wife, knowing her circumstances, offered her more work, which she gladly accepted. It was a happy household, and Mrs Berry was as grateful for the cheerful company she found there as for the extra money.

Mother and daughter fell into a comfortable routine during the next few years. They breakfasted together before the younger woman set off on her bicycle, and Mrs Berry tidied up before going off to her morning's work at the farmhouse. In the afternoon, she did her own housework, washed and ironed, gardened, or knitted and sewed. She frugally made jams and jellies, chutneys and pickles for the store cupboard, and it was generally acknowledged by her neighbours that Mrs Berry could stretch a shilling twice as far as most. The house was bright and attractive, and the door stood open for visitors. No one left Mrs Berry without feeling all the better for her company. Her good sense, her kindness and her courage brought many people to her door.

Mary had been almost thirty when she met Bertie Fuller. He was the nephew of the old lady who kept the Springbourne post office and had come to lodge with her when he took a job at the Caxley printing works.

Even those romantically inclined had to admit that nothing as fantastic as love at first sight engulfed Mary and Bertie. She had never been one to show her feelings and now, at her age, was unlikely to be swept off her feet. Bertie was five years her senior and had been married before. There were no children of this first marriage, and his wife had married again.

The two were attracted to each other and were engaged within three months of their first meeting.

'Well, my dear, you're old enough to know your own mind,' said Mrs Berry, 'and he seems a decent, kindly sort of man, with a steady job. If you'd like to have two rooms here while you look for a house you're both welcome.'

No, the villagers agreed, as they gossiped among themselves, Mary Berry hadn't exactly caught 'a regular heartthrob', but what could you expect at thirty? She was lucky really to have found anyone, and they did say this Bertie fellow was safe at the printing works, and no doubt was of an age to have sown all the wild oats he wanted.

The wedding was as modest as befitted the circumstances, and the pair were married at Caxley registry office, spent their brief honeymoon at Torquay, and returned to share the cottage with old Mrs Berry. It was October 1963 and the autumn was one of the most golden and serene that anyone could recall.

Their first child was due to arrive the following September. Mary gave up her job at the post office in June.

The summer was full of promise. The cottage garden

flowered as never before, and Mary, resting in a deck chair, gazed dreamily at the madonna lilies and golden roses, and dwelt on the happy lot of the future baby. They had all set their hearts on a boy, and Mary was convinced that it would be a son. Blue predominated in the layette that she and Mrs Berry so lovingly prepared.

When her time came she was taken to the maternity wing of the local cottage hospital, and gave birth to a boy, fair and blue eyed like his father. She held him in her arms for a moment before returning him to the nurse's care. In her joy she did not notice the anxious looks the doctor and nurse exchanged. Nor did she realize that her child had been taken from her bed straight to an oxygen tent.

In the morning, they broke the news to her that the boy had died. Mary never forgot the utter desolation that gripped her for weeks after this terrible loss. Her husband and mother together nursed her back to health, but always, throughout her whole life, Mary remembered that longed-for boy with the blue gaze, and mourned in secret.

A daughter, Jane, was born in the spring of 1966, and another, Frances, in 1968. The two little girls were a lively pair, and when the younger one was beginning to toddle, Bertie and Mary set about finding a cottage of their own. Until that time, Mrs Berry had been glad to have them with her. Mary's illness, then her second pregnancy, made her husband and mother particularly anxious. Now, it seemed, the time had come for the young family to look for their own home. Mrs Berry's cottage was becoming overcrowded.

The search was difficult. They wanted to rent a house

to begin with, but this proved to be almost impossible. The search was still on when the annual printing-house outing, called the wayzgoose, took place. Two buses set off for Weymouth carrying the workers and their wives. Mary decided not to go on the day's outing. Frances had a summer cold and was restless, and her mother had promised to go to a Women's Institute meeting in the afternoon. So Bertie went alone.

It was a cloudless July day, warm from the sun's rising until its setting. Mary, pushing the pram along a leafy lane, thought enviously of Bertie and his companions sitting on a beach or swimming in the freshness of the sea. She knew Weymouth from earlier outings and loved its great curved bay. Today it would be looking its finest.

The evening dragged after the children had gone to bed. Usually, the adults retired at ten, for all rose early. On this evening, however, Mrs Berry went upstairs alone, leaving Mary to await Bertie's coming. Eleven o'clock struck, then twelve. Yawning, bemused with the long day's heat, Mary began to lock up.

She was about to lock the front door when she heard a car draw up. Someone rapped upon the door, and when Mary opened it, to her surprise she saw Mr Partridge, the vicar, standing there. His kind old face was drawn with anxiety.

'I'm sorry to appear so late, my dear Mrs Fuller, but a telephone message has just come to the vicarage.'

'Yes?' questioned Mary.

The vicar looked about him in agitation. 'Do you think we might sit down for a moment?'

Mary remembered her manners. 'Of course; I'm so sorry. Come in.'

She led the way into the sitting room, still bewildered.

'It's about Bertie,' began the vicar. 'There's been an accident, I fear. Somewhere south of Caxley. When things were sorted out, someone asked me to let you know that Bertie wouldn't be home tonight.'

'What's happened? Is he badly hurt? Is he dead? Where is he?'

Mary sprang to her feet, her eyes wild.

The vicar spoke soothingly. 'He's in Caxley hospital, and being cared for. I know no more, my dear, but I thought you would like to go there straight away and see him.'

Without a word Mary lifted an old coat from the back of the kitchen door.

The vicar eyed her anxiously. 'Would it not be best to tell Mrs Berry?' he suggested.

She shook her head. 'I'll leave a note.'

He waited while she scribbled briefly upon a piece of paper, and watched her put it in the middle of the kitchen table.

'No point in waking her,' she said, closing the front door softly behind her.

The two set off in silence, too worried to make conversation. The air was heavy with the scent of honeysuckle. Moths glimmered in the beams of the headlights, and fell to their death.

How easily, Mary thought – fear clutching her heart – death comes to living things. The memory of her little son filled her mind as they drove through the night to meet what might be another tragedy.

At the hospital they were taken to a small waiting room. Within a minute, a doctor came to them. There was no need for him to speak. His face told Mary all. Bertie had gone.

The wayzgoose, begun so gaily, had ended in tragedy. The two buses had drawn up a few miles from Caxley to allow the passengers to have a last drink before closing time. They had to cross a busy road to enter the old coaching inn, famed for its hospitality. Returning to the bus, Bertie and a friend waited some time for a lull in the traffic. It was a busy road, leading to the coast, and despite the late hour the traffic was heavy. At last they made a dash for it, not realizing that a second car was overtaking the one they could see. The latter slowed down to let the two men cross, but the second car could not stop in time. Both men were hurled to the ground, Bertie being dragged some yards before the car stopped.

Despite appalling injuries, he was alive when admitted to hospital, but died within the hour. The organizer of the outing, knowing that Mary was not on the telephone, decided to let the local vicar break the news of the accident.

Mr Partridge and poor Mary returned along the dark lanes to the darker cottage, where he aroused Mrs Berry, told her the terrible story and left her trying to comfort the young widow.

If anyone can succeed, Mr Partridge thought as he drove sadly to his vicarage, she can. But oh, the waste of it all! The wicked waste!

Chapter Two

Old Mrs Berry, remembering that dreadful night, shook her head sadly as she washed up her cup and saucer at the sink. The rain still fell in torrents, and a wild wind buffeted the bushes in the garden, sending the leaves tumbling across the grass.

In Caxley it would not be so rough, she hoped. Most of the time her family would be under cover in the shops, but out here, at Shepherds Cross, they always caught the full violence of the weather.

Mrs Berry's cottage was the third one spaced along the road that led to Springbourne. All three cottages were roomy, with large gardens containing gnarled old apple and plum trees. Each cottage possessed ancient hawthorn hedges, supplying sanctuary to dozens of little birds.

An old drovers' path ran at right angles to the cottages, crossing the road by Mrs Berry's house. This gave the hamlet its name, although it was many years since sheep had been driven along that green lane to the great sheep fair at the downland village ten miles distant.

Some thought it a lonely spot, and declared that they 'would go melancholy mad, that they would!' But Mrs Berry, used to remote houses since childhood, was not affected.

She had been brought up in a gamekeeper's cottage in a woodland ride. As a small child she rarely saw anyone strange, except on Sundays, when she attended church with her parents.

She had loved that church, relishing its loftiness, its glowing stained-glass windows and the flowers on the altar. She paid attention to the exhortations of the vicar too, a holy man who truly ministered to his neighbours. From him, as much as from the example of her parents, she learned early to appreciate modesty, courage, and generosity.

When she was old enough to read she deciphered a plaque upon the chancel floor extolling the virtues of a local benefactor, a man of modest means who neverthe-less '*was hospitable and charitable for all his Days*' and who, at his end, left '*the interest of Forty Pounds to the Poor of the parish forever.*'

It was the next line or two which the girl never forgot, and which influenced her own life. They read:

> *Such were the good effects of*
> *Virtue and Oeconomy*
> *Read, Grandeur, and Blush*

Certainly, goodness and thrift, combined with a horror of ostentation and boasting, were qualities which Mrs Berry embodied all the days of her life, and her daughters profited by her example.

Mrs Berry left the kitchen and went to sit by the fire in the living room. It was already growing dark, for the sky was thick with storm clouds, and the rain showed no sign of abating.

Water bubbled in the crack of the window frame, and Mrs Berry sighed. It was at times like this one needed a man about the place. Unobtrusively, without complaint, Stanley and then Bertie had attended to such things as

draughty windows, wobbly door knobs, squeaking floor-boards and the like. Now the women had to cope as best they could, and an old house, about two hundred years of age, certainly needed constant attention to keep it in trim.

Nevertheless, it looked pretty and gay. The Christmas tree, dressed the night before by Jane and Frances – with many squeals of delight – stood on the side table, spangled with stars and tinsel, and bearing the Victorian fairy doll, three inches high, which had once adorned the Christmas trees of Mrs Berry's own childhood. The doll's tiny wax face was brown with age but still bore that sweet expression which the child had imagined was an angel's.

Sprigs of holly were tucked behind the picture frames, and a spray of mistletoe hung where the oil lamp had once swung from the central beam over the dining table.

Mrs Berry leaned back in her chair and surveyed it all with satisfaction. It looked splendid and there was very little more to be done to the preparations in the kitchen. The turkey was stuffed, the potatoes peeled. The Christmas pudding had been made in November and stood ready on the shelf to be plunged into the steamer tomorrow morning. Mince pies waited in the tin, and a splendid Christmas cake, iced and decorated with robins and holly by Mrs Berry herself, would grace the tea table tomorrow.

There would also be a small Madeira cake, with a delicious sliver of green angelica tucked into its top. The old lady had made that for those who, like herself, could not tackle Christmas cake until three or four hours after Christmas pudding. It had turned out beautifully light, Mrs Berry remembered.

She closed her eyes contentedly, and before long, drifted into a light sleep.

Mrs Berry awoke as the children burst into the room. A cold breeze set the Christmas tree ornaments tinkling and rustled the paper chain, which swung above the door.

The little girls' faces were pink and wet, their bangs stuck to their foreheads and glistened with dampness. Drops fell from the scarlet mackintoshes and their woolly gloves were soaked. But nothing could damp their spirits on this wonderful day, and Mrs Berry forbore to scold them for the mess they were making on the rug.

Mary, struggling with the shopping, called from the kitchen.

'Come out here, you two, and get off those wet things! What a day, Gran! You've never seen anything like Caxley High Street. Worse than Michaelmas Fair! Traffic jams all up the road, and queues in all the shops. The Caxley traders will have a bumper Christmas, mark my words!'

Mrs Berry stirred herself and followed the children into the kitchen to help them undress. Mary was unloading her baskets and carrier bags, rescuing nuts and Brussels sprouts which burst from wet paper bags on to the floor, and trying to take off her own sodden coat and headscarf all at the same time.

'I seem to have spent a mint of money,' she said apologetically, 'and dear heaven knows where it's all gone. We'll have a reckon-up later on, but we were that pushed and hurried about I'll be hard put to it to remember all the prices.'

'No point in worrying,' said Mrs Berry calmly. 'If 'tis gone, 'tis gone. You won't have wasted it, I know that, my girl. Here, let's put on the kettle and make a cup of tea. You must be exhausted.'

'Ah! It's rough out,' agreed Mary, sounding relieved now that she had confessed to forgetting the cost of some of her purchases. 'But it's the rush that takes it out of you. If only that ol' bus came back half an hour later 'twould help. As it is, you have to keep one eye on the town clock all the time you're shopping.'

The little girls were delving into the bags, searching for their own secret shopping.

'Now mind what you're at,' said Mary sharply. 'Take

your treasures and put 'em upstairs, and I'll help you pack 'em up when we've had a cup of tea.'

'Don't tell,' wailed Jane. 'It's a secret!'

'A secret!' echoed Frances.

'It still is,' retorted their mother. 'Up you go then, and take the things up carefully. And put on your slippers,' she shouted after them, as they clambered upstairs clutching several small packets against their chests.

'Mad as hatters, they are,' Mary confided to her mother. 'Barmy as March hares – and all because of Christmas!'

'All children are the same,' replied Mrs Berry, pouring boiling water into the teapot, and peering through the silvery steam to make sure it was not overfull. 'You three were as wild as they are, I well remember.' She carried the tray into the living room. 'Could you eat anything?' she asked.

'Not a thing,' said Mary, flopping down, exhausted, into the armchair by the fire, 'and a biscuit will be enough for the girls. They're so excited they won't sleep if they have too much before bedtime.'

'We'll get them upstairs early tonight,' said her mother. 'There are still some presents to pack.'

'We'll be lucky if they go to sleep before nine,' prophesied Mary. 'I heard Jane say she was going to stay awake to see if Father Christmas really does come. She doesn't believe it anymore, you know. I'm positive about that, but she don't let on in case he doesn't come!'

'She's seven,' observed Mrs Berry. 'Can't expect her to believe fairy tales all her life.'

'They've been telling her at school,' said Mary. 'Once they start school they lose all their pretty ways. Frances has only had six months there, but she's too knowing by half.'

The women sipped their tea, listening to the children moving about above them and relishing a few quiet moments on their own.

'They can have a good long time in the bath tonight,' said Mary, thinking ahead, 'then they'll be in trim to go to church with you tomorrow.'

'But wouldn't you like to go?'

'No, Mum. I'll see to the turkey while you're out. The service means more to you than me. Somehow church doesn't seem the same since Bertie went. Pointless, somehow.'

Mrs Berry was too taken aback to comment on this disclosure, and the entry of the children saved her from further conversation on the matter.

Her thoughts were in turmoil as she poured milk into the children's mugs and opened the biscuit tin for their probing fingers.

That unguarded remark of Mary's had confirmed her suspicions. She had watched Mary's growing casualness to religious matters and her increasing absences at church services with real concern. When Stanley died, she had found her greatest consolation in prayer and the teachings of the Church. 'Thy Will Be Done,' it said on the arch above the chancel steps, and for old Mrs Berry those words had been both succour, support and reason.

But, with the death of Bertie, Mary had grown hard, and had rejected a God who allowed such suffering to occur. Mrs Berry could understand the change of heart, but it did not lessen her grief for this daughter who turned her face from the comfort of religious beliefs. Without submission to a divine will, who could be happy? We were too frail to stand and fight alone, but that's what Mary was doing, and why she secretly was so unhappy.

Mrs Berry thrust these thoughts to the back of her mind. It was Christmas Eve, the time for good will to all men, the time to rejoice in the children's pleasure, and to hope that, somehow, the warmth and love of the festival would thaw the frost in Mary's heart.

'Bags not the tap end!' Mrs Berry heard Jane shout an hour later, as the little girls capered naked about the bathroom.

'Mum, she *always* makes me sit the tap end!' complained Frances. 'And the cold tap drips down my back. It's not fair!'

'No grizzling now on Christmas Eve,' said Mary briskly. 'You start the tap end, Frances, and you can change over at halftime. That's fair. You're going to have a nice long bathtime tonight while I'm helping Gran. Plenty of soap, don't forget, and I'll look at your ears when I come back.'

Mrs Berry heard the bath door close, and then open again.

'And stop sucking your facecloth, Frances,' scolded her mother. 'Anyone'd think you're a little baby, instead of a great girl of five.'

The door closed again, and Mary reappeared, smiling.

'They'll be happy for twenty minutes. Just listen to them!'

Two young treble voices, wildly flat, were bellowing 'Away in a manger, no crib for a bed,' to a background of splashes and squeals.

'Did you manage to find some slippers for them?' asked Mrs Berry.

'Yes, Tom's Christine had put them by for me, and I had a quick look while the girls were watching someone try on shoes. There's a lot to be said for knowing people in the shops. They help you out on occasions like this.'

She was rummaging in a deep oilcloth bag as she spoke, and now drew out two boxes. Inside were the slippers. Both were designed to look like rabbits, with shiny black beads for eyes, and silky white whiskers. Jane's pair were blue, and Frances' red. They were Mrs Berry's present to her grandchildren, and she nodded her approval at Mary's choice.

'Very nice, dear, very nice. I'll just tuck a little chocolate bar into each one—'

'There's no need, Mum. This is plenty. You spoil them,' broke in Mary.

'Maybe, but they're going to have the chocolate. Something to wear is a pretty dull Christmas present for a child. I well remember my Aunt Maud – God rest her, poor soul. What a dance she led my Uncle Hubert! She used to give us girls a starched white pinafore every Christmas, and very miserable we thought them.' She shook her head. 'Ungrateful, weren't we? Now I can see it was a very generous present, as well as being useful; but my old grandad gave us two sugar mice, one pink and one white with long string tails, and they were much more welcome, believe me.'

'Like the tangerine and toffees you and Dad used to tuck in the toe of our stockings.' Mary smiled. 'We always rushed for those first before unpacking the rest.

Funny how hungry you are at five in the morning when you're a child!'

'Get me some wrapping paper,' said Mrs Berry briskly, 'and I'll tie them up while those two rascals are safe for ten minutes. They've eyes in the backs of their heads at Christmastime.'

Mary left her mother making two neat parcels. Her wrinkled hands, dappled with brown age spots, were as deft as ever. Spectacles on the end of her nose, the old lady folded the paper this way and that, and tied everything firmly with bright red string.

Mary took the opportunity to smuggle a beautiful pink cyclamen into her own bedroom and hide it behind the curtain on the windowsill. It had cost more than she could really afford, but she had decided to forego a new pair of winter gloves. The old ones could be mended, and who was to notice the much sewn seams in a little place like Shepherds Cross?

She drew the curtains across to hide the plant and to keep out the draught, which was whistling through the cracks of the ancient lattice-paned window. Outside, the wind roared in the branches; a flurry of dead wet leaves flew this way and that as the eddies caught them. The rain slanted down pitilessly, and as a car drove past, the beams of its headlights lit up the shining road where the raindrops spun like silver coins.

She took out from a drawer her own presents for the children. There were two small boxes and two larger ones, and she opened them to have one last look before they were wrapped. In each of the smaller boxes a string of little imitation pearls nestled against a red mock-velvet background. How pretty they would look on the girls' best frocks! Simple, but good, Mary told herself, with satisfaction. As Mum had said, children wanted something more than everyday presents at Christmas, and the two larger boxes *were* rather dull perhaps.

They held seven handkerchiefs, one for each day of the week, with the appropriate name embroidered in the corner. Sensible, and would teach them how to spell too, thought Mary, putting back the lids.

She was just in time, for at that moment the door burst open and she only had a second in which to thrust the boxes back into the drawer, when two naked cherubs skipped in, still wet with bath water.

'What d'you think—' she began, but was cut short by two vociferous voices in unison.

'The water's all gone. Frances pushed out the plug—'

'I never then!'

'Yes, you did! You know you did! Mum, she wriggled it out with her bottom—'

'Well, she never changed ends, like you said. I only wriggled 'cos the cold tap dripped down my back. I couldn't help it!'

'She done it a-purpose.'

'I never. I told you—'

Mary cut short their protestations.

'You'll catch your deaths. Get on back to the bathroom and start to rub dry. Look at your wet foot marks on the floor! What'll Gran say?'

They began to giggle, eyeing each other.

'Let's go down and frighten her, all bare,' cried Jane.

'Don't you dare now!' said their mother, her voice sharpened by the thought of the slippers being wrapped below.

A little chastened by her tone, the two romped out of the room, jostling together like puppies. Mary heard their squeals of laughter from behind the bathroom door, and smiled at her reflection in the glass.

' "Christmas comes but once a year," ' she quoted aloud. 'Perhaps it's as well!'

She followed her rowdy offspring into the bathroom.

Twenty minutes later the two girls sat barefoot on their wooden stools, one at each side of the fire. On their laps they held steaming bowls of bread and milk, plentifully sprinkled with brown sugar.

'You said we could hang up pillow slips tonight,' remarked Jane, 'instead of stockings.'

'I haven't forgotten. There are two waiting on the banisters for you to put at the end of your bed.'

'Will Father Christmas know?' asked Frances anxiously, her eyes wide with apprehension.

'Of course he will,' said their grandmother robustly. 'He's got plenty of sense. Been doing the job long enough to know what's what.'

Mary glanced at the clock.

'Finish up now. Don't hang it out, you girls. Gran and I've got a lot to do this evening, so you get off to sleep as quick as you can.'

'I'm staying awake till he comes,' said Jane firmly.

'Me too,' echoed Frances, scooping the last drop of milk from the bowl.

They went to kiss their grandmother. She held their soft faces against hers, relishing the sweet smell of soap and milk. How dear these two small mortals were!

'The sooner you get to sleep, the sooner the morning will come,' she told them.

She watched them as, followed by Mary, they tumbled up the staircase that opened from the room.

'I *shall* stay awake!' protested Jane. 'I shan't close my eyes, not for *one minute*! I promise you!'

Mrs Berry smiled to herself as she put another log on the fire. She had heard that tale many times before. If she were a betting woman she would lay a wager that those two would be fast asleep within the hour!

But, for once, Mrs Berry was wrong.

Chapter Three

Upstairs, in the double bed, the two little girls pulled the clothes to their chins and continued their day-long conversation.

A nightlight, secure in a saucer on the dressing table, sent great shadows bowing and bending across the sloping ceiling, for the room was crisscrossed with draughts on this wild night from the ill-fitting window and door. Sometimes the brave little flame bent in a sudden blow from the cold air, as a crocus does in a gust of wind, but always it righted itself, continuing to give out its comforting light to the young children.

'Shall I tell you why I'm going to stay awake all night?' asked Jane.

'Yes.'

'Promise to do what I tell you?'

'Yes.'

'Promise *faithfully*? See my finger wet and dry? Cross your heart? *Everything*?'

'Everything,' agreed Frances equably. Her eyelids were beginning to droop already. Left alone, free from the vehemence of her sister, she would have fallen asleep within a minute.

'Then eat your pillow,' demanded Jane.

Frances was hauled back roughly from the rocking sea of sleep.

'You know I can't!' she protested.

'You promised,' said Jane.

'Well, I unpromise,' declared Frances. 'I can't eat a pillow, and anyway what would Mum say?'

'Then I shan't tell you what I was going to.'

'I don't care,' replied Frances untruthfully.

Jane, enraged by such lack of response and such wanton breaking of solemn vows, bounced over on to her side, her back to Frances.

'It was about Father Christmas,' she said hotly, 'but I'm not telling you now.'

'He'll come,' said Frances drowsily.

This confidence annoyed Jane still further.

'Maybe he won't then! Tom Williams says there isn't a Father Christmas. That's why I'm going to stay awake. To see. So there!'

Through the veils of sleep which were fast enmeshing her, Frances pondered upon this new problem. Tom Williams was a big boy, ten years old at least. What's more, he was a sort of cousin. He should know what he was talking about. Nevertheless . . .

'Tom Williams don't always speak the truth,' answered Frances. In some ways, she was a wiser child than her sister.

Jane gave an impatient snort.

'Besides,' said Frances, following up her point, 'our teacher said he'd come. She don't tell lies. Nor Mum, nor Gran.'

These were powerful allies, and Jane was conscious that Frances had some support.

'Grownups hang together,' said Jane darkly. 'Don't forget we saw *two* Father Christmases this afternoon in Caxley. What about that then?'

'They was men dressed up,' replied Frances stolidly. 'Only *pretend* Father Christmases. It don't mean there isn't a real one as 'll come tonight.'

A huge yawn caught her unawares.

'You stay awake if you want to,' she murmured, turning her head into the delicious warmth of the uneaten pillow. 'I'm going to sleep.'

Secure in her faith, she was asleep in five minutes, but Jane, full of doubts and resentful of her sister's serenity, threw her arms above her head, and, gripping the rails of the brass bedstead, grimly began her vigil. Tonight she would learn the truth!

Downstairs, the two women assembled the last few presents that needed wrapping on the big table.

They made a motley collection. There were three or four pieces of basketwork made by Mary, who was neat with her fingers, and these she eyed doubtfully.

'Can't see myself ever making a tidy parcel of these flower holders,' she remarked. 'D'you think just a Christmas tag tied on would be all right?'

Mrs Berry surveyed the hanging baskets thoughtfully.

'Well, it always looks a bit slapdash, I feel, to hand over something unwrapped. Looks as though you can't be bothered—'

'I can't,' said Mary laconically.

'But I see your point. We'd make a proper pig's ear of the wrapping paper trying to cover those. You're right, my girl. Just a tag.'

Mary sat down thankfully and drew the packet of tags towards her. The presents were destined for neighbours, and the tags seemed remarkably juvenile for the elderly couples who were going to receive the baskets. Father Christmas waved from a chimney pot, a golliwog danced a jig, two pixies bore a Christmas tree, and a cat carried a Christmas pudding. Only two tags measured up to Mary's requirements, a row of bells on one and a red candle on the other. Ah well, she told herself, someone must make do with the pixies or the cat, and when you came to think of it the tags would be on the back of the fire this time tomorrow, so why worry? She wrote diligently.

Outside the wind still screamed, rattling the window, and making the back door thump in its frame. The curtains stirred in the onslaught, and now and again a little puff of smoke came into the room from the log fire, as the wind eddied round the chimney pot.

Mrs Berry looked up from the jar of honey she was wrapping.

'I'll go and see if the rain's blowing in under that door at the back.'

She went out, causing a draught that rustled the wrapping paper and blew two of Mary's tags to the floor. Mrs Berry was gone for some minutes, and returned red-faced from stooping.

'A puddle a good yard wide,' she puffed. 'I've left that old towel stuffed up against the crack. We'll have to get a new sill put on that threshold, Mary. It's times like this we miss our menfolk.'

Mary nodded, not trusting herself to speak. Hot tears pricked her eyes, but she bent lower to her task, so that her mother should not see them. How was it, she wondered, that she could keep calm and talk about her loss, quite in control of her feelings, for nine tenths of the time, and yet a chance remark, like this one, pierced her armour so cruelly? Poor Gran! If only she knew! Better, of course, that she did not. She would never forgive herself if she thought she had caused pain.

Unaware of the turmoil in her daughter's mind, Mrs Berry turned her attention to a round tin of shortbread.

' 'Pon my word,' she remarked. 'I never learn! After all these years, you'd think I'd know better than to pick a round tin instead of a square 'un. I'll let you tackle this, Mary. It's for Margaret and Mary Waters. They're good to us all through the year, taking messages and traipsing round with the parish magazine in all weathers.'

Mary reached across for the tin, then checked. The eyes of the two women met questioningly. Above the sound of the gale outside they had heard the metallic clink of their letter box.

'I'll go,' said Mary.

An envelope lay on the damp mat. She opened the door, letting in a rush of wind and rain and a few sodden

leaves. There was no one to be seen, but in the distance
Mary thought she could see the bobbing light of a flash-
light. To shout would have been useless. To follow, in her
slippers, idiotic. She pushed the door shut against the
onslaught, and returned to the light with the envelope.

'For you, Mum,' she said, handing over the glistening
packet.

Mrs Berry withdrew a Christmas card, bright with
robins and frosted leaves, and two embroidered white
handkerchiefs.

'From Mrs Burton,' said Mrs Berry wonderingly. 'Now, who'd have thought it? Never exchanged presents before, have we? What makes her do a thing like this, I wonder? And turning out too, on such a night. Dear soul, she shouldn't have done it. She's little enough to spare as it is.'

'You did feed her cat and chickens for her while she was away last summer,' said Mary. 'Perhaps that's why.'

'That's only acting neighbourly,' protested Mrs Berry. 'No call for her to spend money on us.'

'Given her pleasure, I don't doubt,' answered Mary. 'The thing is, do we give her something back? And, if so, what?'

It was a knotty problem. Their eyes ranged over the presents before them, already allotted.

'We'll have to find *something*,' said Mrs Berry firmly. 'What about the box of soap upstairs?'

'People are funny about soap,' said Mary. 'Might think it's a hint, you know. She's none too fond of washing, nice old thing though she is.'

They racked their brains in silence.

'Half a pound of tea?' suggested Mrs Berry at last.

'Looks like charity,' replied Mary.

'Well, I wouldn't say no to a nice packet of tea,' said Mrs Berry with spirit. 'What about one of our new tea towels then?'

'Cost too much,' said Mary. 'She'd mind about that.'

'I give up then,' said Mrs Berry. 'You think of something. I must say these last-minute surprises are all very fine, but they do put you to some thinking.'

She tied a final knot round the honey pot and rose to her feet again.

'Talking of tea, what about a cup?'

'Lovely,' said Mary.

'Shall I cut us a sandwich?'

'Not for me. Just a cup of tea.'

The old lady went out, and Mary could hear the clattering of cups and saucers, and the welcome tinkle of teaspoons. Suddenly, she felt inexpressibly tired. She longed to put her head down among the litter on the table and fall asleep. Sometimes she thought Christmas was more trouble than it was worth. All the fuss and flurry, then an empty purse just as the January bills came in. If only she had her mother's outlook! She still truly loved Christmas. She truly celebrated the birth of that God who walked beside her every hour of the day. She truly loved her neighbour – even that dratted Mrs Burton, who was innocently putting them to such trouble.

Mrs Berry returned with the round tin tray bearing the cups and saucers and the homely brown teapot clad in a knitted tea cosy. Her face had a triumphant smile.

'I've thought of something. A bottle of my blackcurrant wine. How's that? She can use it for her cough, if she don't like it for anything better. What say?'

'Perfect!' said Mary. In agreement at last, they sipped their tea thankfully.

Still awake upstairs, Jane heard the chinking of china and the voices of her mother and grandmother. Beside her, Frances snored lightly, her pink mouth slightly ajar, her lashes making dark crescents against her rosy cheeks.

Jane's vigil seemed lonelier and bleaker every minute. What's more, she was hungry, she discovered. The thought of the blue biscuit tin, no doubt standing by the teacups below, caused her stomach to rumble. Cautiously, she slid her skinny legs out of bed, took a swift glance at the two empty pillowcases draped expectantly one each end of the brass bed rail, and crept to the door.

The wind was making so much noise that no one heard the latch click, or the footsteps on the stairs. The child opened the bottom door, which led directly into the living room, and stood blinking in the light like a little owl caught in the sunshine.

'Mercy me!' gasped Mrs Berry, putting down her cup with a clatter. 'What a start you gave me, child!'

'Jane!' cried her mother. 'What on earth are you doing down here?' Her voice was unusually sharp. Surprised and startled, she could have shaken the child in her exasperation.

'I'm hungry,' whispered Jane, conscious of her un-popularity.

'You had a good supper,' said Mary shortly. 'Time you was asleep.'

'Let her come by the fire for a minute,' pleaded Mrs Berry. 'Shut that door, my dear. The draught fairly cuts through us. Want a cup of tea, and a biscuit?'

The child's face lit up. 'Shall I fetch a cup?'

'Not with those bare feet,' said Mary. 'I'll get your mug, and then you go straight back to bed as soon as you're finished. Your gran's too good to you.'

She hurried kitchenwards, and the child sat on the rag rug smiling at the flames licking the log. It was snug down here. It was always snug with Gran.

She put a hand on the old lady's knee. 'Mum's cross,' she whispered.

'She's tired. Done a lot today, and you know you should really be abed, giving her a break.'

They always hang together, these grownups, thought Jane rebelliously; but she took the mug of weak tea gratefully, and the top biscuit from the tin when it was offered, even though it was a Rich Tea and she knew there were Ginger Nuts further down.

'Is Frances asleep?' asked Mary.

'Yes. I couldn't get off.'

'You told me you didn't intend to,' replied her mother. 'Trying to see Father Christmas, silly girl. As though he'll come if you're awake! The sooner you're asleep the sooner he'll come!'

Torn with doubts, the child looked swiftly up into her grandmother's face. It told her nothing. The familiar kind smile played around the lips. The eyes looked down at her as comfortingly as ever.

'Your mother's right. Drink up your tea, and then snuggle back into bed. I'll come and tuck you up this time.'

Jane tilted her mug, put the last fragment of biscuit into her mouth, and scrambled to her feet.

'Whose presents are those?' she said, suddenly aware of the parcels on the table.

'Not yours,' said Mary.

'Neighbours',' said her grandmother in the same breath. 'You shall take some round for us tomorrow. And I want you to carry a bottle of wine very carefully to Mrs Burton. Can you do it, do you think?'

The child nodded, hesitated before her mother, then kissed her warmly on the cheek.

'You hussy!' said Mary, but her voice was soft, and the

child saw that she was forgiven. Content at last, she followed her grandmother's bulk up the narrow stairs.

The flame of the night light was burning low in the little hollow of its wax. The shadows wavered about the room as the old woman and the child moved towards the bed.

'Now, no staying awake, mind,' whispered Gran, in a voice that brooked no argument. 'I don't know who's been stuffing your head with nonsense, but you can forget it. Get off to sleep, like Frances there. You'll see Father Christmas has been, as soon as you wake up.'

She kissed the child, and tucked in the bedclothes tightly.

Jane listened to her grandmother's footsteps descending the creaking stairs, sighed for her lost intentions, and fell, almost instantly, into a deep sleep.

CHAPTER FOUR

'My! That was a lucky escape,' said Mrs Berry. 'Good thing we hadn't got out those pillowcases!'

Two pillowcases, identical to those hanging limply upstairs, had been hidden behind the couch in the cottage parlour for the last two days. Most of the presents were already in them. A doll for each, beautifully dressed in handsewn clothes, joint presents from Mary and her mother; a game of Ludo for Frances and Snakes and Ladders for Jane; and a jigsaw puzzle apiece. All should provide plenty of future pleasure.

The American aunt had sent two little cardigans, pale pink and edged with silver trimming – far more glamorous than anything to be found in the Caxley shops. The less well-off aunt at Taunton had sent bath salts for both, which, Mary knew, would enchant the little girls. There were also gifts from kind neighbours – a box of beads, a toy shop (complete with tiny metal scales), and several tins of sweets, mint humbugs and homemade toffee among them.

A stocking, waiting to be filled with small knick-knacks, lay across each pillowcase. As soon as the children were safely asleep, the plan had been to substitute the full pillowcases for the empty ones.

'I thought she might reappear,' admitted Mary. 'She's twigged, you know, about Father Christmas. Some of the children at school have let it out.'

'She won't come down again, I'm certain,' replied Mrs

Berry comfortingly. 'Let's fill up the stockings, shall we? We can put the last-minute odds and ends in when we carry up the pillowcases.'

Mary nodded agreement and went to the parlour, returning with the limp stockings. They were a pair of red and white striped woollen ones, once the property of the vicar's aunt, and reputedly kept for skating and skiing in her young days. Mary had bought them at a jumble sale, and each Christmas since they had appeared to delight the little girls.

From the dresser drawer, Mrs Berry collected the store of small treasures that had been hidden there for the last week or so. A few wrapped sweets, a curly stick of barley sugar, a comb, a tiny pencil and pad, a brooch and a handkerchief followed the tangerines that stuffed the toe of each stocking. Then, almost guiltily, Mrs Berry produced the final touch – two small wooden Dutch dolls.

'Saw them in the market at Caxley,' she said, 'and couldn't resist them, Mary. They reminded me of a family of Dutch dolls I had at their age. They can amuse themselves dressing them up.'

The dolls were tucked at the top, their shiny black heads and stiff wooden arms sticking out attractively. The two women gazed at their handiwork with satisfaction.

'Well, that's that!' said Mrs Berry. 'I'm just going to clear away this tray and tidy up in the kitchen, and I shan't be long out of bed.'

'I'll wait till I'm sure those two scallywags are really asleep,' answered Mary. 'I wouldn't put it past our Jane to pretend, you know. She's stubborn when she wants to be, and she's real set on finding out who brings the presents.'

The hands of the clock on the mantelpiece stood at ten o'clock. How the evening had flown! Mary tidied the table, listening to the gale outside, and the sound of her mother singing in the kitchen.

She suddenly remembered her own small presents upstairs still unwrapped and crept aloft to fetch them. The door of the girls' room was ajar. She tiptoed in and looked down upon the sleeping pair. It seemed impossible that either of them could be feigning sleep, so rhythmically were they breathing. What angels they looked!

She made her way downstairs and swiftly wrapped up the necklaces and handkerchiefs. The very last, she thought thankfully! Just a tag for Mum's cyclamen, and I can write that and tie it on when I go to bed.

She selected the prettiest tag she could find, and slipped it into her skirt pocket to take upstairs.

Mrs Berry reappeared, carrying the glass of water that she took to her bedroom every night.

'I'll be off then, my dear. Don't stay up too long. You must be tired.'

She bent to kiss her daughter.

'The girls have gone off, I think, but I'll give them another ten minutes to make sure.'

'See you in the morning, then, Mary,' said the old lady, mounting the stairs.

Mary raked the hot ashes from the fire and swept up the hearth. She fetched the two bulging pillowcases and put the stockings on top of them. Then she sat in the old armchair and let exhaustion flood through her. Bone-tired, she confessed to herself. Bone-tired!

Above her she could hear the creaking of the floor-boards as her mother moved about, then a cry and hasty footsteps coming down the stairs.

The door flew open and Mrs Berry, clad in her flannel nightgown, stood, wild eyed, on the threshold.

'Mum, what's the matter?' cried Mary, starting to her feet.

'A mouse!' gasped Mrs Berry, shuddering uncontrollably. 'There's a mouse in my bedroom!'

The two women gazed at each other, horror struck. Mary's heart sank rapidly, but she spoke decisively.

'Here, you come by the fire, and let's shut that door. The girls will be waking up.'

She pushed up the armchair she had just vacated and Mrs Berry, still shuddering, sat down thankfully.

'You'll catch your death,' said Mary, raking a few bright embers together and dropping one or two shreds of dry bark from the hearth on to the dying fire. 'You ought to have put on your dressing gown.'

'I'm not going up there to fetch it!' stated Mrs Berry flatly. 'I know I'm a fool, but I just can't abide mice.'

'I'll fetch it,' said Mary, 'and I'll set the mousetrap too while I'm there. Where did it go?'

Mrs Berry shivered afresh.

'It ran under the bed, horrible little thing! You should've seen its tail, Mary! A good three inches long! It made me cry out, seeing it skedaddle like that.'

'I heard you,' said Mary, making for the kitchen to get the mousetrap.

Mrs Berry drew nearer to the fire, tucking her voluminous nightgown round her bare legs. A cruel draught

whistled in from the passage, but nothing would draw her from the safety of the armchair. Who knows how many more mice might be at large on a night like this?

Mary, her mouth set in a determined line, reappeared with the mousetrap and went quietly upstairs. She returned in a moment, carrying her mother's dressing gown and slippers.

'Now you wrap up,' she said coaxingly, as if she were addressing one of her little daughters. 'We'll soon catch that old mouse for you.'

'I'm ashamed to be so afeared of a little creature,' confessed Mrs Berry, 'but there it is. They give me the horrors, mice do, and rats even worse. Don't ask me why!'

Mary knew from experience this terror of her mother's. She confronted other hazards of country life with calm courage. Spiders, caterpillars, bulls in fields, adders on the heath, any animals in pain or fury found old Mrs Berry completely undaunted. Mary could clearly remember her mother dealing with a dog that had been run over and writhed, demented with pain, not far from their cottage door. It had savaged two would-be helpers, and a few distressed onlookers were wondering what to do next when Mrs Berry approached and calmed the animal in a way that had seemed miraculous. But a mouse sent her flying, and Mary knew, as she found some wood to replenish the fire, that nothing would persuade her mother back to the bedroom until the intruder had been dispatched.

She settled herself in the other armchair, resigned to another twenty minutes or more of waiting. She longed desperately for her bed, but could not relax until her mother was comfortably settled. She listened for sounds from above – the click of the mousetrap that would release her from her vigil, or the noise of the children waking and rummaging for the pillowcases, wailing at the nonappearance of Father Christmas.

But above the noise of the storm outside, it was difficult to hear anything clearly upstairs. She pushed the two telltale pillowcases under the table, so that they were hidden from the eyes of any child who might enter unannounced, and leaned back with her eyes closed.

Invariably, Bertie's dear face drifted before her when she closed her eyes, but now, to her surprise and shame, another man's face smiled at her. It was the face of one of Bertie's workmates. He too had been one of the party on that tragic wayzgoose, and had written to Mary and her mother soon after the accident. She had known him from childhood. Rather a milksop, most people said of Ray Bullen, but Mary liked his gentle ways and thought none the less of him because he had remained a bachelor.

'Some are the marrying sort, and some aren't,' she had replied once to the village gossip who had been speculating upon Ray's future. Mary was all too conscious of the desire of busybodies to find her a husband in the months after Bertie's death. They got short shrift from Mary, and interest waned before long.

'Too sharp tongued by half,' said those who had been lashed by it. 'No man in his senses would take her on, and them two girls too.'

Here they were wrong. One or two men had paid attention to Mary, and would have welcomed some advances on her side. But none were forthcoming. Truth to tell, Mary was in such a state of numbed shock for so long that very little affected her.

But Ray's letter of condolence had been kept. There was something unusually warm and comforting in the simple words. Here was true sympathy. It was the only letter that had caused Mary to weep and, weeping, to find relief.

She saw Ray very seldom, for their ways did not cross. But that afternoon in Caxley he had been at the bus stop when she arrived laden with baskets and anxious about the little girls amidst the Christmas traffic. He had taken charge of them all so easily and naturally – seeing them on to the bus, disposing of the parcels, smiling at the children and wishing them all well at Christmas – that it was not until she was halfway to Shepherds Cross that

Mary realized that he had somehow contrived to give the little girls a shilling each. Also, she realized with a pang, he must have missed his own bus, which went out about the same time as theirs.

She supposed, leaning back now in the armchair, that her extreme tiredness had brought his face before her tonight. It was not a handsome face, to be sure, but it was kind and gentle, and, from all she heard, Ray Bullen had both those qualities as well as strong principles. He was a Quaker, she knew, and she remembered a little passage about Quakers from the library book she was reading. Something about them 'making the best chocolate and being very thoughtful and wealthy and good.' It had amused her at the time, and though Ray Bullen could never be said to be wealthy, he was certainly thoughtful and good.

She became conscious of her mother's voice, garrulous in her nervousness.

'It's funny how you can sense them when you're frightened of them. Not that I had any premonition tonight, I was too busy thinking about getting those pillowcases safely upstairs. But I well remember helping my aunt clear out her scullery when I was a child. No older than Frances, I was then, and she asked me to lift a little old keg she kept her flour in. And, do you know, I began to tremble, and I told her I just couldn't do it. "There's a mouse in there!" I told her.

'She was so wild. "Rubbish!" she stormed. She was a quick-tempered woman, red haired and plump, and couldn't bear to be crossed. "Pick it up at once!"

'And so I did. And when I looked inside, there *was* a mouse, dead as a doornail and smelling to high heaven! I dropped that double quick, you can be sure, and it rolled against a bottle of cider and smashed it to smithereens. Not that I waited to see it happen. I was down at the end of the garden, in the privy with the door bolted. She couldn't get at me there!'

Mary had heard the tale many times, but would not have dreamed of reminding her mother of the fact. It was her mother's way, she realized, of apologizing for the trouble she was causing.

Mrs Berry hated to be a nuisance, and now, with Mary so near to complete exhaustion, she was being the biggest nuisance possible, the old lady told herself guiltily. Why must that dratted mouse arrive in her bedroom on Christmas Eve?

In the silence that had fallen there was the unmistakeable click of a mousetrap. Mary leaped to her feet.

'Thank God!' said Mrs Berry in all seriousness. Panic seized her once more. 'Don't let me see it, Mary, will you? I can't bear to see their tails hanging down.'

'I'll bring the whole thing down in the wastepaper basket,' promised Mary.

But when she returned to the apprehensive old lady waiting below, she had nothing in her hand.

'He took a nibble and then got away,' she said. 'We'll have to wait a bit longer. I've set it a mite finer this time.'

'I wish you had a braver mother,' said Mrs Berry forlornly. Mary smiled at her, and her mother's heart turned over. The girl looked ten years younger when she smiled. She didn't smile enough, that was the trouble. Time she got over Bertie's loss. There was a time for grieving, and a time to stop grieving. After all, she was still young and, smiling as she was now, very pretty too.

Conversation lapsed, and the two tired women listened to the little intimate domestic noises of the house, the whispering of the flames, the hiss of a damp log, the rattle of the loose-fitting window. Outside, the rain fell down pitilessly. Mrs Berry wondered if the rolled-up towel was stemming the flood at the back door but was too tired to go and see.

She must have dozed, for when she looked at the clock it was almost eleven. Mary was sitting forward in her chair, eyes fixed dreamily on the fire, miles away from Shepherds Cross.

She stirred as her mother sat up.

'I'll go and see if we've had any luck.'

Up the stairs she tiptoed once more, and returned almost immediately. She looked deathly pale with tiredness, and Mrs Berry's heart was moved.

'Still empty. He's a fly one, that mouse. What shall we do?'

Mrs Berry took charge with a flash of her old energy and spirit.

'You're going to bed, my girl. You're about done in, I can see. I'll stay down here for the night, for go up to that bedroom I simply cannot do!'

'But, Mum, it's such a beast of a night! You'd be better off in bed. Just wake me if the trap springs and I'll come and see to it. It's no bother, honest.'

'No, Mary, you've done more than enough, and tomorrow's a busy day. I'll be all right here in the armchair. 'Tisn't the first time I've slept downstairs, and the storm don't trouble me.'

Mary looked doubtfully at the old lady but could see that her mind was made up.

'All right then, Mum. I'll go and fetch your eiderdown and pillow, and see you've got enough firing handy.'

Yet again she mounted the stairs, while Mrs Berry made up the fire and bravely went to have a quick look at the towel by the back door. No more water had seeped in, so presumably the defenses were doing their work satisfactorily. She returned to the snug living room to find Mary plumping up the pillow.

'Now, you're sure you're all right?' she asked anxiously. 'If I hear that trap go off before I get to sleep, shall I call you?'

'No, my dear. You'll be asleep as soon as your head hits the pillow tonight. I can see that. I shall settle here and be perfectly happy.'

Mary retrieved the pillowcases, kissed her mother's

forehead, and went to the staircase for the last time that night.

'Sleep well,' she said, smiling at her mother, who by now was wrapped in the eiderdown. 'You look as snug as a bug in a rug, as the children say.'

'Good night, Mary. You're a good girl,' said her mother, watching the door close behind her daughter.

Nearly half-past eleven, thought Mrs Berry. What a time to go to bed! Ten o'clock was considered quite late enough for the early risers of Shepherds Cross.

She struggled from her wrappings to turn off the light and to put a little small coal on the back of the fire. The room was very pretty and cosy by the flickering firelight. There was no sound from upstairs. All three of them, thought Mrs Berry, would be asleep by now, and that wretched mouse still making free in her own bedroom, no doubt.

Ah well, she was safe enough down here, and there was something very companionable about a fire in the room when you were settling down for the night.

She turned her head into the feather-filled pillow. Outside the storm still raged and she could hear the rain drumming relentlessly upon the roof and the road. It made her own comfort doubly satisfying.

God pity all poor travellers on a night like this, thought Mrs Berry, pulling up the eiderdown. 'There's one thing: I shan't be awake long, storm or no storm.'

She sighed contentedly and composed herself for slumber.

CHAPTER FIVE

B ut tired though she was, Mrs Berry could not get to sleep. Perhaps it was the horrid shock of the mouse, or the unusual bustle of Christmas that had overtired her. Whatever the reason, the old lady found herself gazing at the rosy reflection of the fire on the ceiling, her mind drifting from one inconsequential subject to the next.

The bubbling of rain forcing its way through the crack of the window reminded her of the more ominous threat at the back door. Well, she told herself, that towel was standing up to the onslaught when she looked a short while ago. It must just take its chance. In weather like this, usual precautions were not enough. Stanley would have known what to do. A rolled-up towel wouldn't have been good enough for him! Some sturdy carpentry would have made sure that the back door was completely weather-proof.

Mrs Berry sighed and thought wistfully of their manless state. Two good husbands gone, and no sons growing up to take their place in the household! It seemed hard, but the ways of God were inscrutable and who was to say why He had taken them first?

She thought of her first meeting with Stanley, when she was nineteen and he two years older. She had been in service then at the vicarage. Her employer was a predecessor of Mr Partridge's, a bachelor who held the living of Fairacre for many years. He was a vague, saintly man, a great Hebrew scholar who had written a number of learned commentaries on the minor prophets of the Old Testament. His parishioners were proud of his scholarship but, between themselves, admitted that he was 'only ninepence in the shilling' when it came to practical affairs.

Nevertheless, the vicarage was well run by a motherly old body who had once been nurse to a large family living in a castle in the next county. This training stood her in good stead when she took over the post of housekeeper to the vicar of Fairacre. She was methodical, energetic and abundantly kind. When a vacancy occurred for a young maid at the vicarage, Mrs Berry's parents thought she would be extremely lucky to start work in such pleasant surroundings. They applied for the post for their daughter, then aged thirteen.

Despite her lonely upbringing in the gamekeeper's cottage, Amelia Scott, as she was then, was a friendly child, anxious to help and blessed with plenty of common sense. The housekeeper realized her worth, and trained her well, letting her help in the kitchen as well as learning the secrets of keeping the rest of the establishment sweet and clean.

She thrived under the old lady's tuition, and learned by her example to respect the sterling qualities of her employer. He was always ready to help his neighbours, putting aside his papers to assist anyone in trouble, and welcoming all – even the malodorous vagrants who 'took advantage of him', according to the housekeeper – into his study to give them refreshment of body and spirit.

One bright June morning, when the dew sparkled on the roses, Amelia heard the chinking of metal on stone, and leaned out of the bedroom window to see two men at work on one of the buttresses of St Patrick's church. The noise continued all the morning, and as the sun rose in the blue arc of a cloudless sky, she wondered if the master would send her across with a jug of cider to wash down the men's dinners, as he often did. Then she remembered that he was out visiting at the other end of the parish. The housekeeper too was out on an errand. She was choosing the two plumpest young fowls, now running about in a neighbour's chicken run, for the Sunday meal.

Amelia was helping Bertha, the senior housemaid, to clean out the attics when they heard the ringing of the back-door bell.

'You run and see to that,' said Bertha, her arms full of derelict pillows. 'I'll carry on here.'

Amelia sped downstairs through the shadows and sunlight that streaked the faded blue carpet, and opened the back door.

A young man, with thick brown hair and very bright dark eyes, smiled at her apologetically.

He held his left hand, which was heavily swathed in a red spotted handkerchief, in his right one, and dark stains showed that he was bleeding profusely.

'Been a bit clumsy,' he said. 'My tool slipped.'

'Come in,' said Amelia, very conscious that she was alone to cope with this emergency. She led the way to the scullery and directed the young man to the shallow slate sink.

'Put your hand in that bowl,' she told him, 'and I'll pump some water. It's very pure. We've got one of the deepest wells in the parish.'

It was certainly a nasty gash, and the pure water, so

warmly recommended by Amelia, was soon cloudy with
blood.

'Keep swilling it around,' directed Amelia, quite enjoying her command of the situation, 'while I get a bit of rag
to bandage it.'

'There's no need miss,' protested the young man. 'It's
stopping. Look!'

He held out the finger, but even as he did so, the blood
began to well again. Amelia took one look and went to the
bandage drawer in the kitchen dresser. Here, old pieces
of linen sheeting were kept for just such an emergency,
and the housekeeper's pot of homemade salve stood
permanently on the shelf above.

No one quite knew what the ingredients of this cure-all were, for the recipe's secret was jealously guarded, but goose grease played a large part in it, along with certain herbs that the old lady gathered from the hedgerows. During the few years of Amelia's residence at the vicarage she had seen this salve used for a variety of ailments, from chilblains to the vicar's shaving rash, and always with good results.

She returned now with the linen and the pot of ointment. The young man still smiled, and Amelia smiled back.

'Let me wrap it up,' she said. 'Let's put some of this stuff on first.'

'What's in it?'

'Nothin' to hurt you.' Amelia assured him. 'It's good for everything. Cured some spots I had on my chin quicker 'n lightning.'

'I don't believe you ever had spots,' said the young man gallantly. He held out the wounded finger, and Amelia twisted the strip round and round deftly, cutting the end in two to make a neat bow.

'There,' she said with pride, 'now you'll be more comfortable.'

'Thank you, miss. You've been very kind.'

He picked up the bloodied handkerchief.

'Leave that there,' said Amelia, 'and I'll wash it for you.'

'No call to trouble you with that,' said the young man. 'My ma will wash it when I get back.'

'Blood stains need soaking in cold water,' Amelia told him, 'and the sooner the better. I'll put it to soak now, then wash it out.'

'Well, thank you. We're working on the church for the rest of the week. Can I call in tomorrow to get it?'

Amelia felt a glow of pleasure at the thought of seeing him again, so soon. She liked his thick hair, his quick eyes, and his well-tanned skin – a proper nut-brown man, and polite too. Amelia looked at him with approval.

'I'll be here,' she promised.

'My name's Berry,' said the young man. 'Stanley Berry. What's yours?'

'Amelia Scott.'

'Well, thank you, Amelia, for a real good job. I must be getting back to work or I'll get sacked.'

She watched him cross the garden in the shimmering heat, the white bandage vivid against the brown background of his skin and clothes. He paused in the gateway leading to the churchyard, waving to her.

Delighted, she waved back.

'You've taken your time,' grumbled Bertha, when she returned to the attic. She looked at Amelia's radiant face shrewdly. 'Who'd you see down there? Prince Charming?'

Amelia forbore to answer, but thought that Bertha seemed to have guessed correctly.

The next morning the young man called to collect his handkerchief. Amelia had washed and ironed it with extreme care, and had put it carefully on the corner of the dresser to await its owner.

He carried a bunch of pink roses, and at the sight of them Amelia felt suddenly shy.

'You shouldn't have bothered,' she began, but the young man hastily put her at ease.

'My ma sent them, to thank you for what you did, and for washing the handkerchief. She said you're quite right. She'd have had the devil's own job to get out the stain if I'd left it till evening.'

Amelia took the bunch and smelled them rapturously.

'Please do thank her for them. They're lovely. I'll put them in my room.'

Stanley gave her a devastating smile again.

'I picked them,' he said gently.

'Then, thank you too,' said Amelia, handing over the handkerchief.

They stood in silence for a moment, gazing at each other, loath to break the spell of this magic moment.

'Best be going,' said Stanley, at length. He gave a gusty sigh, which raised Amelia's spirits considerably, and set off, stuffing the handkerchief in his pocket. He had not gone more than a few steps when he halted and turned.

'Can I come again, Amelia?'

'*Please*,' said Amelia, with rather more fervour than a well-bred young lady should have shown. But then Amelia always spoke her mind.

There was no looking back, no hesitation, no lovers' quarrels. From that first meeting they trod a smooth, blissfully happy path of courtship. They were both even-tempered, considerate people, having much the same background and, most important of all, the same sense of fun. There were no family difficulties, and the wedding took place on a spring day as sunny as that on which they had first met.

They lived for the first few years at Beech Green, in a small cottage thatched by Dolly Clare's father, who was one of their neighbours. The first two girls were born there, and then the house at Shepherds Cross was advertised to let. It was considerably bigger than their first house, and although it meant a longer cycle ride for Stanley, this did not deter him.

Here Mary was born. They had hoped for a boy this time, but the baby was so pretty and good that the accident of her sex was speedily forgotten.

Amelia and Stanley were true homemakers. Amelia's early training at the vicarage had given her many skills. She could make frocks for the children, curtains, bedspreads, and rag rugs as competently as she could make a cottage pie or a round of shortbread. The house always looked as bright as a new pin, and Stanley saw to it that any stonework or woodwork was in good repair. They shared the gardening and it was Mrs Berry's pride that they never needed to buy a vegetable.

The longing for a son never left Amelia. She liked a man about the place, and it was doubly grievous when Stanley died so suddenly. She lost not only her lover and husband, but the comfort of all that a shared life meant.

Mary's Bertie brought back to the cottage the feeling of comfort and reliability. The birth of her grandson had meant more to Mrs Berry than she cared to admit. It was the continuance of male protection that subconsciously she needed. The baby's early death was something she mourned as deeply as Mary and Bertie had.

A piece of wood fell from the fire, and Mrs Berry stirred herself to reach for the tongs and replace it. Not yet midnight! She seemed to have been lying there for hours, dreaming of times passed.

Poor Stanley, poor Bertie, poor baby! But what a

blessing the two little girls were! Mary knew how to bring up children. Plenty of fun, but no nonsense when it came to doing as they were told. Say what you will, thought old Mrs Berry, it didn't do people any harm to have a little discipline. You could cosset them too much, and give in to their every whim, and what happiness did that bring?

She remembered neighbours in the early days of her marriage at Beech Green. They were an elderly pair when their first child arrived, a pale sickly little fellow called, much to the ribaldry of some of the Beech Green folk, Clarence.

The baby was only put out into the garden on the warmest days, and then he was so swaddled in clothes that his normally waxen complexion was beaded with perspiration. The doctor harangued the doting mother; friends and neighbours, genuinely concerned for the child's health, proffered advice. Nothing was of any avail. Clarence continued to be smothered with love.

Not surprisingly, he was late in walking and talking. When he was at the toddling stage, his mother knitted him a long pair of reins in scarlet wool, and these were used in all his walks abroad. Mrs Berry herself had seen the child tethered by these same red reins to the fence near the back door, so that his mother could keep an eye on him as she worked.

He was a docile child, too languid to protest against his restrictions and, never having known freedom, he accepted his lot with a sweet meekness that the other mothers found pathetic.

Clarence reached the age of six, still cosseted, still adored, still forbidden the company of rough playmates who might harm him. But one bleak December day he fell ill with some childish infection that a normal boy would have thrown off in a day or two. Clarence drooped and died within the week, and the grief of the parents was terrible to see.

Poor Clarence and his red reins! thought Mrs Berry, looking back over the years. She thought of him as 'the sweet dove' that died, in Keats' poem. Long, long ago she had learned it, chanting with the other children at the village school, and still, seventy years on, she could remember it.

> *I had a dove, and the sweet dove died;*
> *And I have thought it died of grieving:*
> *Oh, what could it grieve for? Its feet were tied*
> *With a silken thread of my own hand's weaving;*
> *Sweet little red feet! Why should you die—*
> *Why should you leave me, sweet bird, why?*
> *You lived alone in the forest tree,*
> *Why, pretty thing, would you not live with me?*
> *I kissed you oft and gave you white peas;*
> *Why not live sweetly, as in the green trees?*

Yes, that was Clarence! 'Tied with a silken thread' of his poor mother's weaving. The stricken parents had moved away soon after the tragedy, and very little was heard of them, although someone once said that the mother had been taken to the madhouse, years later, and was never fit to be released.

Thank God, thought Mrs Berry, turning her pillow, that children were brought up more sensibly these days. She thought of Mary's two vivacious daughters, their glossy hair and round pink cheeks, their exuberance, their inexhaustible energy. Well, they were quiet enough at the moment, though no doubt they would wake early and fill the house with their excitement.

Mrs Berry rearranged the eiderdown, turned her cheek into the pillow, and, thanking God for the blessing of a family, fell asleep at last.

Chapter Six

An unaccustomed sound woke the old lady within an hour. She slept lightly these days, and the stirring of one of her granddaughters or the mewing of a cat was enough to make her instantly alert.

She lay listening for the sound again. The wind still moaned and roared outside, the rain pattered fitfully against the windowpane, and the fire whispered as the wood ash fell through the bars of the grate.

It was a metallic noise that had roused her. What could it be? It might possibly be caused by part of the metal trellis which she and Mary had erected against the front porch to aid the growth of a new rose. Could it have blown loose?

But she could have sworn that the sound was nearer at hand, somewhere inside the house. It was not the welcome click of the mousetrap at its work. Something downstairs . . .

She sat upright in the chair. The fire had burned very low, and she leaned forward to put a little more wood on it, taking care to make no noise. Her ears strained for a repetition of the sound.

Now she thought she could hear a slight scuffling noise. A bird? Another mouse? Her heart began to beat quickly. And then the tinny sound again, as though a lid were being lifted from a light saucepan, or a cake tin. Without doubt, someone was in the kitchen!

Mrs Berry sat very still for a minute. She felt no fear,

but she was cautious. She certainly did not intend to rouse the sleeping family above. Whoever it was, Mrs Berry felt quite capable of coping with him. Some rough old tramp probably, seeking a dry billet from the storm and, if left alone, on his way before the house stirred at daybreak. Mrs Berry began to feel justifiable annoyance at the thought of some wastrel making free with her accommodation, and, what was more to the point, rifling the larder.

She bent to pick up the poker from the hearth. There was only one chance in ten that she would need to use it, but it was as well to be armed. It gave her extra confidence, and should the man be so silly as to show fight, then she would lay about him with energy and leave him marked.

Tightening her dressing-gown cord round her ample waist, Mrs Berry, poker in hand, moved silently to the door of the living room. This door, then a short passage, and then the kitchen door needed to be negotiated before she came face to face with her adversary. Mrs Berry determined to take the obstacles at a rush, catching the intruder before he had a chance to make his escape.

For one brief moment, before she turned the doorknob, the battered face of an old woman swam into Mrs Berry's mind. The photograph had been given pride of place in the local paper only that week, and showed the victim of some young hooligans who had broken into her pathetic home to take what they could. Well, Mrs Berry told herself sturdily, such things might happen in a town. It wouldn't occur in a little homely place like Shepherds Cross! She had dealt with plenty of scoundrels in her day, and knew that a stout heart was the best defence against bullies. Right would always triumph in the end, and no good ever came of showing fear!

She took a deep breath, a firmer grip on the poker, and flung open the door. Four quick determined steps took her to the kitchen door. She twisted the knob, and pushed the door open with her foot.

There was a stifled sound, something between a sob and a scream, a scuffle, and an unholy clattering as a large tin fell upon the tiles of the kitchen floor.

Mrs Berry switched on the light with her left hand, raised the poker menacingly in her right, and advanced upon her adversary.

Upstairs, Jane stirred. She lay still for a minute or two, relishing the warmth of her sister's back against hers, and the delicious warm hollow in which her cheek rested.

Then she remembered, and sat up. It was just light enough to see that the two empty pillowcases had vanished. She crept carefully out of bed, and went to the foot. There on the floor stood two beautifully knobbly pillowcases, and across each lay an equally beautiful striped stocking.

He had been! Father Christmas had been! Wild excitement was followed by a wave of shame. And she had not seen him! She had fallen asleep, after all her resolutions! It would be a whole year now before she could put Tom Williams' assertion to the test again. She shivered in the cold draught that blew under the door.

Her hands stroked the bulging stocking lovingly. There was the tangerine, there were the sweets, and this must be a dear little doll at the top. If only morning would come! She did not intend to undo the presents now. She would wait until Frances woke.

She crept back to bed, shivering with cold and excitement. She thrust her head into the hollow of her pillow again, leaned back comfortably against her sister, sighed rapturously at the thought of joys to come, and fell asleep again within a minute.

*

Mrs Berry's stern gaze, which had been directed to a point about six feet from the ground, at a height where her enemy's head should reasonably have been, now fell almost two feet to rest upon a pale, wretched urchin dressed in a streaming wet raincoat.

At his feet lay Mrs Berry's cake tin, luckily right way up, with her cherished Madeira cake exposed to the night air. The lid of the cake tin lay two yards away, where it had crashed in the turmoil.

'*Pick that up!*' said Mrs Berry in a terrible voice, pointing imperiously with the poker.

Snivelling, the child did as he was told, and put it on the table.

'*Now the lid!*' said Mrs Berry with awful emphasis. The boy sidled nervously towards it, his eyes fixed fearfully upon the menacing poker. He retrieved it and replaced it fumblingly, Mrs Berry watching the while.

The floor was wet with footmarks. The sodden towel had been pushed aside by the opening door. Mrs Berry remembered with a guilty pang that she had forgotten to lock the door amidst the general excitement of Christmas Eve.

She looked disapprovingly at the child's feet, which had played such havoc upon the kitchen tiles. They were small, not much bigger than Jane's, and clad in a pair of sneakers that squelched with water every time the boy moved. He had no socks, and his legs were mauve with cold and covered with goose pimples.

Mrs Berry's motherly heart was smitten, but no sign of softening showed in her stern face. This boy was nothing more than a common housebreaker and thief. A minute

more and her beautiful Madeira cake, with its artistic swirl of angelica across the top, would have been demolished – gulped down by this filthy ragamuffin.

Nevertheless, one's Christian duty must be done.

'Take off those shoes and your coat,' commanded Mrs Berry, 'and bring them in by the fire. I want to know more about you, my boy.'

He struggled out of them, and picked them up in a bundle in his arms. His head hung down and little droplets of water ran from his bangs down his cheeks.

Mrs Berry unhooked the substantial striped roller towel from the back of the door and motioned to the boy to precede her to the living room.

'And don't you dare to make a sound,' said Mrs Berry

in a fierce whisper. 'I'm not having everyone woken up by a rapscallion like you.'

She prodded him in the back with the poker and followed her reluctant victim to the fireside.

He was obviously completely exhausted and was about to sink into one of the armchairs, but Mrs Berry stopped him.

'Oh, no you don't, my lad! Dripping wet, as you are! You towel yourself dry before you mess up my furniture.'

The boy took the towel and rubbed his soaking hair and wet face. Mrs Berry studied him closely. Now that she had time to look at him, she saw that the child was soaked to the skin. He was dressed in a T-shirt and grey flannel shorts, both dark with rainwater.

'Here, strip off,' commanded Mrs Berry.

'Eh?' said the boy, alarmed.

'You heard what I said. Take off those wet clothes. Everything you've got on.'

The child's face began to pucker. He was near to tears.

'Lord, boy,' said Mrs Berry testily, 'I shan't look at you. In any case, I've seen plenty of bare boys in my time. Do as you're told, and I'll get you an old coat to put on while your things dry.'

She stood a chair near the fire and hung the child's sodden coat across the back of it. His small sneakers were placed on the hearth, on their sides, to dry.

The boy slowly divested himself of his wet clothing, modestly turning his back towards the old lady.

She thrust more wood upon the fire, looking at the blaze with satisfaction.

'Don't you dare move till I get back,' warned Mrs Berry, making for the kitchen again. An old duffel coat of Jane's hung there. It should fit this skinny shrimp well enough. Somewhere too, she remembered, a pair of shabby slippers, destined for the next jumble sale, were tucked away.

She found them in the bottom of the shoe cupboard and returned to the boy with her arms full. He was standing shivering by the fire, naked but for the damp towel round his loins.

He was pathetically thin. His shoulder blades stuck out like little wings, and every rib showed. His arms were like sticks, his legs no sturdier, and they were still, Mrs Berry noticed, glistening with water.

'Sit down, child,' she said, more gently, 'and give me that towel. Seems you don't know how to look after yourself.'

He sat down gingerly on the very edge of the armchair, and Mrs Berry knelt before him rubbing energetically at the skinny legs. Apart from superficial mud, Mrs Berry could see that the boy was basically well cared for. His toe nails were trimmed, and his scarred knees were no worse than most little boys'.

She looked up into the child's face. He was pale with fatigue and fright, his features sharp, the nose prominent; his small mouth, weakly open, disclosed two slightly projecting front teeth. Mouselike, thought Mrs Berry, with an inward shudder, and those great ears each side of the narrow pointed face added to the effect.

'There!' said Mrs Berry. 'Now you're dry. Put your feet in these slippers and get this coat on you.'

The child did as he was told in silence, fumbling awkwardly with the wooden toggle fastenings of the coat.

'Here, let me,' said Mrs Berry, with some exasperation.

Deft herself, she could not abide awkwardness in others. The boy submitted to her ministrations, holding up his head meekly, and gazing at her from great dark eyes as she swiftly fastened the top toggles.

'Now pull that chair up close to the fire, and stop shivering,' said Mrs Berry briskly. 'We've got a lot to talk about.'

The boy did as he was bidden, and sat with his hands held out to the blaze. By the light of the fire, Mrs Berry observed the dark rings under the child's eyes and the open drooping mouth.

'Close your mouth and breathe through your nose,' Mrs Berry told him. 'Don't want to get adenoids, do you?'

He closed his mouth, swallowed noisily, and gave the most appallingly wet sniff. Mrs Berry made a sound of disgust, and struggled from her chair to the dresser.

'Blow your nose, for pity's sake,' she said, offering him several paper handkerchiefs. He blew noisily, and then sat, seemingly exhausted by the effort, clutching the damp tissue in his skinny claw.

'Throw it on the back of the fire, child,' begged Mrs Berry. 'Where on earth have you been brought up?'

He looked at her dumbly and, after a minute, tossed the handkerchief towards the fire. He missed and it rolled into the hearth by the steaming sneakers.

Mrs Berry suddenly realized that she was bone tired, it would soon be one o'clock, and that she wished the wretched child had chosen some other house to visit at such an hour. Nevertheless, duty beckoned, and she girded herself to the task.

'You know what you are, don't you?' she began. The boy shook his head uncomprehendingly.

'You are a burglar and a thief,' Mrs Berry told him. 'If I handed you over to the police, you'd get what you deserve.'

At this the child's dark eyes widened in horror.

'Yes, you may well look frightened,' said Mrs Berry, pressing home the attack. 'People who break into other people's homes and take their things are nothing more than common criminals and have to be punished.'

'I never took nothin',' whispered the boy. With a shock, Mrs Berry realized that these were the first words that she had heard him utter.

'If I hadn't caught you when I did,' replied Mrs Berry severely, 'you would have eaten that cake of mine double quick! Now wouldn't you? Admit it. Tell the truth.'

'I was hungry,' said the child. He put his two hands on his bare knees and bent his head. A tear splashed down upon the back of one hand, glittering in the firelight.

'And I suppose you are still hungry?' observed Mrs Berry, her eyes upon the tear that was now joined by another.

'It's no good piping your eye,' she said bracingly, 'though I'm glad to see you're sorry. But whether 'tis for what you've done, or simply being sorry for yourself, I just don't know.'

She leaned forward and patted the tear-wet hand.

'Here,' she said, more gently, 'blow your nose again and cheer up. I'll go and get you something to eat, although you know full well you don't deserve it.' She struggled from her chair again.

'It won't be cake, I can tell you that,' she told him flatly. 'That's for tea tomorrow – today, I suppose I

should say. Do you realize, young man, that it's Christmas Day?'

The boy, snuffling into his handkerchief, looked bewildered but made no comment.

'Well, what about bread and milk?'

A vision of her two little granddaughters spooning up their supper – days ago, it seemed, although it was only a few hours – rose before her eyes. Simple and nourishing, and warming for this poor, silly, frightened child!

'Thank you,' said the boy. 'I like bread and milk.'

She left him, still sniffing, but with the second paper handkerchief deposited on the back of the fire as instructed.

'Not a sound now,' warned Mrs Berry, as she departed. 'There's two little girls asleep up there. And their ma. All tired out and need their sleep. Same as I do, for that matter.'

She cut a thick slice of bread in the cold kitchen. The wind had not abated, although the rain seemed less violent, Mrs Berry thought, as she waited for the milk to heat. She tidied the cake tin away, wondering whether she would fancy the cake at tea time after all its vicissitudes. Had those grubby paws touched it, she wondered?

She poured the steaming milk over the bread cubes, sprinkled it well with brown sugar and carried the bowl to the child.

He was lying back in the chair with his eyes shut, and for a moment Mrs Berry thought he was asleep. He looked so defenceless, so young, and so meekly mouse-like, lying there with his pink-tipped pointed nose in the air, that Mrs Berry's first instinct was to tuck him up in her dressing gown and be thankful that he was at rest.

But the child struggled upright, and held out his skinny hands for the bowl and spoon. For the first time he smiled, and although it was a poor, wan thing as smiles go, it lit up the boy's face and made him seem fleetingly attractive.

Mrs Berry sat down and watched him attack the meal. It was obvious he was ravenously hungry.

'I never had no tea,' said the child, conscious of Mrs Berry's eyes upon him.

'Why not?'

The boy shrugged his shoulders.

'Dunno.'

'Been naughty?'

'No.'

'Had too much dinner then?'

The child gave a short laugh.

'Never get too much dinner.'

'Was your mother out then?'

'No.'

The boy fell silent, intent upon spooning the last delicious morsels from the bottom of the bowl.

'I don't live with my mother,' he said at last.

'With your gran?'

'No. A foster mother.'

Mrs Berry nodded, her eyes never moving from the child's face. What was behind this escapade?

'Where have you come from?' she asked.

The boy put the empty bowl carefully in the corner of the hearth.

'Tupps Hill,' he answered.

Tupps Hill! A good two or three miles away! What a journey the child must have made, and in such a storm!

'Why d'you want to know?' said the boy, in a sudden panic. 'You going to send the police there? They don't know nothin' about me runnin' off. Honest! Don't let on, madam, please, madam!'

The 'madam' amused and touched Mrs Berry. Was this how he had been told to address someone in charge of an institution, or perhaps a lady magistrate at some court proceedings? This child had an unhappy background, that seemed certain. But why was he so scared of the police?

'If you behave yourself and show some sense,' said Mrs Berry, 'the police will not be told anything at all. But I want to know more about you, young man.'

She picked up the bowl.

'Would you like some more?'

'Can I?' said the child eagerly.

'Of course,' said Mrs Berry, resting the bowl on one hip and looking down at the boy.

'What's your name?'

'Stephen.'

'Stephen what?'

'It's not my foster mother's name,' said the boy evasively.

'So I imagine. What is it, though?'

'It's Amonetti. Stephen Amonetti.'

Mrs Berry nodded slowly, as things began to fall into place.

'So you're Stephen Amonetti, are you? I think I knew your dad some years ago.'

She walked slowly from the room, sorting out a rag bag of memories, as she made her way thoughtfully towards the kitchen.

Chapter Seven

Amonetti!

Pepe Amonetti! She could see him now, as he had first appeared in Beech Green during the final months of the last war. He was a very young Italian prisoner of war, barely twenty, and his dark curls and sweeping black eyelashes soon had all the village girls talking.

He was the youngest of a band of Italian prisoners allotted to Jesse Miller, who then farmed a large area at Beech Green. He was quite irrepressible, bubbling over with the joy of living – doubly relishing life, perhaps, because of his short time on active service.

As he drove the tractor, or cleared a ditch, or slashed back a hedge, he sang at the top of his voice, or chattered in his pidgin English to any passer-by.

The girls, of course, did not pass by. The string of compliments, the flashing glances, the expressive hands, slowed their steps. Pepe, with his foreign beauty, stood out from the local village boys like some exotic orchid among a bunch of cottage flowers. In theory, he had little spare time for such dalliance. In practice, he managed very well, with a dozen or more willing partners.

The young lady most in demand at Beech Green at that time was a blonde beauty called Gloria Jarvis.

The Jarvises were a respectable couple with a string of flighty daughters. Gloria was one of the youngest, and had learned a great deal from her older sisters. The fact that the air base nearby housed several hundred eager young Americans generous with candy, cigarettes and nylon stockings had hastened Gloria's progress in the art of making herself charming.

As was to be expected, 'them Jarvis girls' were considered by the upright members of the community to be 'a fair scandal, and a disgrace to honest parents.' Any man, however ill-favoured or decrepit, was reckoned to be in danger from their wiles, and as soon as Pepe arrived at Beech Green it was a foregone conclusion that he would fall prey to one of the Jarvis harpies.

'Not that he'll put up much of a fight,' observed one middle-aged lady to her neighbour. 'Got a roving eye himself, that lad.'

'Well,' replied her companion indulgently, 'you knows what these foreigners are! Hot blooded. It's all that everlasting sun!'

'My Albert was down with bronchitis and chilblains all through the Italian campaign,' retorted the first lady. 'No, you can't blame the climate for their goings-on. It's just that they're made that way, and them Jarvis girls won't cool their blood, that's for sure.'

It was not long before Pepe's exploits, much magnified in conversations among scandalized matrons, were common knowledge in the neighbourhood, and it was Gloria Jarvis who was named as being the chief object of his attentions.

Gloria may have lost her heart to Pepe's Latin charms, but she did not lose her head. An Italian prisoner of war had little money to spend on a girl, and Gloria continued to see a great deal of her American admirers who spent more freely. Those of them who knew about Pepe dismissed the affair good-naturedly. Gloria was a good-time girl, wasn't she? So what?

Pepe, on the other hand, resented the other men's attentions, and became more and more possessive as time went by. He certainly had more hold over the wayward Gloria than his rivals, and though she tossed her blonde Edwardian coiffure and pretended indifference, Gloria was secretly a little afraid of Pepe's passion.

The war ended in 1945, a few months after their first meeting, and Pepe elected to stay on in England as a farm worker. By this time, a child was on the way, and Gloria and Pepe were married at the registry office in Caxley.

The child, a girl, had Pepe's dark good looks. A blond boy, the image of his mother, appeared a year later, and the family began to be accepted in Beech Green. Pepe continued to work for Jesse Miller and to occupy one of his cottages.

For a few years all went well, and then Pepe vanished. Gloria and the two children had a hard time of it, although Jesse Miller kindheartedly allowed them to continue to live in the cottage. It was during these difficult days that Mrs Berry had got to know Gloria better.

She was vain, stupid and a slattern, but she was also abandoned and in despair. Mrs Berry helped her to find some work at a local big house, and now and again looked after the children to enable Gloria to go shopping or to visit the doctor. The old Jarvises were dead, by now, and the older sisters were little help.

Mrs Berry showed Gloria how to make simple garments for the children, taught her how to knit and, more useful still, how to choose the cheap cuts of meat and cook them so that a shilling would stretch to its farthest limit.

Happily married herself, Mrs Berry urged Gloria to

find Pepe and make it up, if only for the sake of the family. But it was two years before the errant husband was traced, and another fifteen months before he could be persuaded to return.

He had found work in Nottingham, and came back to Beech Green just long enough to collect Gloria and the children, their few poor sticks of furniture and their clothes. They left for Nottingham one grey December day, but Pepe had found time to call at Mrs Berry's and to thank her for all she had done.

Handsomer than ever, Pepe had stood on her doorstep, refusing to come in, his eyes shy, his smile completely disarming. No one, least of all Mrs Berry, could have remained hostile to this winning charmer with his foreign good manners.

'I did nothing – no more than any other neighbour,' Mrs Berry told him. 'But now it's your concern, Pepe. You see you treat her right and make a fresh start.'

'Indeed, yes. I do mean to do that,' said Pepe earnestly. He thrust his hand down inside his greatcoat and produced a ruffled black kitten, which he held out to Mrs Berry with a courtly bow.

'Would you please to accept? A thank you from the Amonettis?'

Mrs Berry was taken aback but rallied bravely. She knew quite well that the kitten was their own, and that they could not be bothered to take it with them to their new home. But who could resist such a gesture? And who would look after the poor little waif if she did not adopt it?

She took the warm furry scrap and held it against her face.

'Thank you, Pepe. I shall treasure it as a reminder of you all. Good luck now, and mind my words.'

For some time after this Mrs Berry heard nothing of the Amonettis. The kitten, named Pepe after its donor, grew up to be a formidable mouser and was much loved by the Berry family. Years later, someone in Caxley told Mrs Berry that Pepe had vanished yet again, and that Gloria had returned to live with a sister in the county town twenty miles away. Whilst there, she had had one last brief reconciliation with Pepe, but within a week there had been recriminations, violence and police action. After this, Pepe had vanished for good, and it was generally believed that this time he had returned to Italy.

The outcome of that short reunion must be Stephen,

Mrs Berry thought to herself, as she stood in her draughty kitchen preparing the boy's meal. Gloria's present circumstances she knew from hearsay. She continued to live in one room of her sister's house and was what Mrs Berry still thought of as 'a woman of the streets.' No wonder that the boy had been taken into the care of the local authority. His mother, though to be pitied in some ways, Mrs Berry told herself charitably, was no fit person to bring up the boy, and heaven above knows what the conditions of the sister's house might be! Those Jarvis girls had all been first-class sluts, and no mistake!

Mrs Berry picked up the tray and carried it back to the fireside.

The child's smile was stronger this time.

'You are very kind,' he said, with a touch of his father's grace, reaching hungrily for the food.

She sat back in the armchair and watched the boy. Now that he had eaten and was getting warm, the pinched look, which sharpened his mouselike features, had lessened. His cheeks glowed pink and his lustrous dark eyes glanced about the room as he became more relaxed. Given time, thought Mrs Berry, this boy could become as bewitching as his father. But, at the moment, he was unhappy. What could have sent the child out into such a night as this? And furthermore, what was to be done about it?

Mrs Berry bided her time until the second bowlful had vanished, then took up the poker. The boy looked apprehensive, but Mrs Berry, ignoring him, set the poker about its legitimate business of stirring the fire into a blaze, and then replaced it quietly.

'Now,' she said, in a businesslike tone, 'you can just

213

explain what brings you into my house at this time of night, my boy.'

There was a long pause. In the silence, the clock on the mantel shelf struck two and a cinder clinked into the hearth. The wind seemed to have shifted its quarter slightly, for now it had found a crevice by the window and moaned there as if craving for admittance.

'I'm waiting,' said Mrs Berry ominously.

The boy's thin fingers fidgeted nervously with the toggle fastenings. His eyes were downcast.

'Not much to tell,' he said at last, in a husky whisper.

'There must be plenty,' replied Mrs Berry, 'to bring you out from a warm bed on Christmas Eve.'

The child shook his head unhappily. Tears welled up again in the dark eyes.

'Now, that's enough of that!' said the old lady. 'We've had enough waterworks for one night. If you won't tell me yourself, you can just answer a few questions. And I want the truth, mind!'

The boy nodded, and wiped his nose on the back of his hand. Mrs Berry pointed in silence to the paper hankies beside him. Meekly, he took one and dried his eyes.

'You say you live at Tupps Hill?'

The child nodded.

'Who with?'

A look of fear crept over the mouselike face.

'You tellin' the police?'

'Not if you tell me the truth.'

'I live at Number Three. With Mrs Rose.'

'Betty Rose? And her husband's Dick Rose, the road-man?'

'That's right.'

Mrs Berry digested this information, whilst the child took advantage of the lull in the interrogation to turn his shoes in the hearth. They were drying nicely.

Mrs Berry tried to remember all she knew about the Roses. They had been married some time before her own girls, she seemed to recall, and Betty's mother had been in good service at Caxley. Other than that, she knew little about them, except that they were known to be a respectable honest pair and regular churchgoers. Dick Rose was a slow methodical fellow, who would never rise above his present job of road sweeper in Caxley, from what Mrs Berry had heard.

'Any children?' she asked.

'Two!' replied the boy. He looked sulky. Was this the clue? Was the child jealous for some reason?

'How old?'

'Jim's eleven, two years older 'n me. Patsy's eight, nearly nine. A bit younger 'n me.'

That would be about right, thought Mrs Berry, trying to piece the past together from her haphazard memories, and the child's reluctant disclosures.

'You're lucky to live with the Roses,' observed the old lady, 'and to have the two children for company.'

The boy gave a sniff, but whether in disgust or from natural causes it was impossible to say.

'You get on all right?'

'Sometimes. Patsy tags on too much. Girls is soppy.'

'They've usually got more sense than boys,' retorted Mrs Berry, standing up for her own sex. 'You notice it isn't Patsy who's run out into a storm and got into trouble.'

The child stuck out his lower lip mutinously but said nothing. The drenched raincoat was now steaming steadily, and Mrs Berry turned it on the back of the chair. The boy's thin T-shirt, which had been hanging over the fire screen, was now dry, and Mrs Berry smoothed it neatly into shape on her knee before folding it.

'Patsy's got a watch,' said the boy suddenly.

'Has she now?'

'So's Jim. They both got watches. Patsy and Jim.'

'For Christmas, do you mean?'

'No, no!' said the child impatiently. 'Patsy had hers in the summer, for her birthday. Jim had his on his birthday. Last month it was.'

'They were lucky.'

She waited for further comment, but silence fell again. The boy was clearly upset about something, some injustice connected with the watches, some grievance that still rankled. His fingers plucked nervously at a piece of loose cotton on the hem of the duffel coat. His face was thunderous. Pepe's Latin blood was apparent as his son sat there brooding by the fire.

'They're their own kids, see?' said the boy, at length. 'So they give 'em watches. I reckon my real mum'd give me one – just like that, if I asked her.'

Light began to break through the dark puzzle in Mrs Berry's mind.

'Do you know where she is?'

The child looked up, wide eyed with amazement.

'Course I do! She's with me auntie. I sees her once a month. She says she'll have me back, soon as she's got a place of her own. Ain't no room at Auntie's, see?'

Mrs Berry did see.

'I want to know more about these watches. When is your birthday?'

'Second of February.'

'Well, you might be lucky too, and get a watch then.'

'That's what *they* say!' said the boy with infinite scorn in his voice. His head was up now, his eyes flashing. The mouse had become a lion.

'If they means it,' he went on fiercely, 'why don't they let me have it for Christmas? That's what I asked 'em.'

'And what did they say?'

'Said as there was too much to buy anyway at Christmas. Couldn't expect a big present like a watch. I'd 'ave to wait and see.'

'Fair enough,' commented Mrs Berry. The Roses had obviously done their best to explain matters to the disappointed child.

'No, it ain't fair enough!' the child burst out. 'Dad Rose, 'e gets extra money Christmastime – a bonus they calls it. *And* all his usual pay. They could easy afford one little watch. The other two've got theirs. Why should I have to wait? I'll tell you why!'

He leaned forward menacingly. Mrs Berry could see why Pepe had had such a hold over poor stupid Gloria Jarvis. Those dark eyes could be very intimidating when they flashed fire.

'Because I'm only the foster kid, that's why! They gets paid for havin' me with 'em, but they won't give me a watch, same as their own kids 've got. They don't care about me, that's the truth of it!'

The tears began to flow again, and Mrs Berry handed him a paper hanky in silence. It was coming out now – the

whole, sad, silly, simple little story. Soon she would know it all.

'I thought about it when I got to bed,' sniffed Stephen Amonetti, mopping his eyes. 'Soon as Jim was asleep, I crept out. They never heard me go. They was watching the telly. Never heard nothing. I knows the way.'

'Where to?'

'Me mum, of course. She'd understand. I bet she'd give me a watch for Christmas, *and* let me stay with her too, if she knowed how I was feeling. Anyway, you wants your own folk at Christmastime. I fair hates the Roses just now.'

He blew his nose violently, threw the hanky to the back of the fire as instructed, and flopped back in the chair, with a colossal shuddering sigh. The duffel coat fell apart, displaying his skinny bare legs. His hands drooped from the arms of the chair.

Mrs Berry stooped to put another log on the fire, before beginning her lecture. That done, she settled back in the armchair.

'As far as I can see,' she began severely, 'you are a thoroughly silly, spoiled little boy.'

She glanced across at her visitor and saw that she was wasting her breath.

Utterly exhausted, his pink mouse nose pointing towards the ceiling and pink mouse mouth ajar, Mrs Berry's captive was deep in slumber.

CHAPTER EIGHT

Upstairs in her draughty bedroom Mary stirred. Some faint noise had penetrated the thick folds of sleep that wrapped her closely. Too tired to open her eyes or to sit up, she tried bemusedly to collect her thoughts.

Could she have heard voices? She remembered that her mother was below. Perhaps she had turned on the little radio set for company, she told herself vaguely.

Should she go and inspect the mousetrap? The bed was seductively warm, her limbs heavy with sleep. To stir outside was impossible. Besides, she might wake the children as well as her mother.

Exhausted, she turned over, relishing the comfort of her surroundings after the bustle of the day. She began to slip back into unconsciousness, and her last remembrance of Christmas Eve was the sight of Ray Bullen's smile as he hoisted young Frances on to the bus.

With a feeling of warm contentment, Mary drifted back to sleep.

Old Mrs Berry rearranged the eiderdown and put her tired head against the back of the chair. Through half-closed eyes she surveyed her visitor.

He was snoring slightly, and Mrs Berry's maternal instinct made her want to approach the boy and quietly close his mouth. It was shameful the way some people let their children grow up to be mouth breathers – leading the way to all sorts of infections in later life, besides encouraging snoring, an unnecessary complication to a shared bedroom. Why, Mrs Berry could recall, from when she was in service, many a shocking case among the gentry of couples agreeing to separate bedrooms simply on account of snoring!

However, on this present occasion, Mrs Berry proposed to let sleeping dogs lie. The child was not her permanent responsibility. But Betty Rose ought to look into the matter herself, and quickly, before the habit grew worse.

Her thoughts hovered round the events that had led to the boy's presence under her roof. As far as she could judge, the boy was sensibly cared for by the Roses, who seemed to have tackled the child's grievance sympathetically.

There was no doubt in Mrs Berry's mind that the child was far better off where he was than with that fly-by-night mother of his. As for thinking that she would have him back permanently to live with her – well, that was just wishful thinking on the child's part. The local authority would not allow that, especially in the sordid circumstances in which Gloria now appeared to live and work.

Stephen Amonetti! Mrs Berry mused, her eyes still on her visitor. He would not be an easy child to bring up, with Pepe and Gloria as parents. She pitied the Roses, and commended them for having the pluck to take on this pathetic outcome of a mixed marriage. He would need a firm hand, and plenty of affection too, to right the wrongs the world had done him. It could not be easy for the Roses, trying to be fair to their own two and to fit this changeling into their family.

She remembered Pepe's quick jealousy of Gloria's earlier rivals. Plainly, this child was as quick to resentment as his father had been. She remembered the fury in those dark eyes as the boy spoke of the watches. That smouldering jealousy was a legacy from his Latin father. The thoughtlessness, culminating in the flight from home, careless of the feelings of others, was a legacy from his casual mother.

This boy was going to be a handful, unless someone pulled him to his senses, thought Mrs Berry. The Roses, respectable people though they were, might well be too gentle with the child, too ineffectual, although they apparently were doing their best to cope with this cuckoo in their nest. After all, Dick Rose left home early in the morning and was late back at night. It would fall upon Betty's shoulders, this responsibility, and with two children of her own to look after the task might be too great for her.

The child had been thinking on the wrong lines for too long, Mrs Berry told herself. He had harboured grievances, resented authority, and indulged in self-pity. The old lady, with the strong principles instilled by her Victorian upbringing, condemned such wrong-headedness roundly. That the child was the victim, to a certain extent, of his circumstances, she was ready to concede, but the matter did not end there. She was heartily sick of the modern theories that condoned wrongdoing on the grounds that the wrongdoers were to be pitied and not blamed.

Every individual, she firmly believed, had the freedom of choice between good and evil. If one were so wicked, or thoughtless, or plain stupid enough to choose to do evil, then one must be prepared to take the consequences. Children, naturally, had to be trained and helped to resist temptation and to choose the right path, but to consider them as always in the right, as so many people nowadays seemed to do, was to do them a disservice, thought old Mrs Berry.

Her own children had been brought up with clear standards. Little Amelia Scott had learned the virtues early, from the plaque in the church extolling modesty and economy, from her upright parents, and from the strict but kindly teachings of the village schoolteachers, the Scriptures and the vicar of the parish. These stood her in good stead when she became a mother.

She had also been told of the things which were evil: lying, boasting, stealing, cruelty and loose living and thinking. It seemed to Mrs Berry that in these days evil was ignored. Did modern parents and teachers think that by burying their heads in the sand, evil would vanish? It had to be faced today, as bravely as it always had been in the past. It was there, plain for all to see, in the deplorable accounts of murder, bloodshed, violence and exploitation appearing in newspapers and shown on every television screen. The trouble was, thought Mrs Berry, that too often it was shrugged off as 'an aspect of modern living', when it should have been fought with the sword of righteousness, as she and her generation had been taught to do.

It was a great pity that the seven deadly sins were not explained to the young these days. There, asleep in the chair, was the victim of one of them – Envy. Had he been brought up to recognize his enemies in time, young Stephen might have been safely asleep in his own bed, instead of lying there caught in a web of his own weaving.

For, one had to face it, Mrs Berry told herself, this self-indulgence in envy and self-pity had led the boy to positive wrongdoing. He was, in the eyes of the law and all right-thinking people, a burglar and a would-be thief.

He was also guilty of disloyalty to the Roses, who were doing their best to bring him up. And he had completely disregarded the unhappiness this flight might cause them.

All this she intended to make clear to the child as soon as he awoke. But there was a further problem – a practical one. How could she get the child home again without involving her own family or the Roses?

Would they have missed him yet? Would they have rung the police? As soon as the child woke, she would try and find out the usual practice at night in the Roses' house. Would they on Christmas Eve have put the children's presents on their beds, as she and Mary had done? If so, would they have noticed that the boy was missing from their son's side?

All this must be discovered. Meanwhile, it was enough that the boy was resting. She too would close her eyes for a catnap. They both needed strength to face what was before them.

She dropped, thankfully, into a light doze.

The boy woke first. Bending to feel his drying shoes, he knocked the poker into the hearth. This small clatter roused the old lady.

She was alert at once, as she always was when she woke up, despite her age.

The clock stood at twenty minutes past three, and

although the wind still moaned at the window, there seemed to be no sound of rain pattering on the pane. The worst of the storm appeared to be over.

Mrs Berry felt the raincoat. It was practically dry. She carefully turned the sleeves inside out and rearranged the garment so that it had the full benefit of the fire's heat.

It was very cosy in the room. Refreshed by her nap, the old lady looked with approval at the two red candles on the mantelpiece waiting to be lit at teatime – today, Christmas Day, the day they had prepared for, for so long.

The Christmas tree sparkled on the side table. The paper chains, made by the little girls' nimble fingers, swayed overhead and the holly berries glimmered as brightly as the fire itself.

'Merry Christmas!' said Mrs Berry to the boy.

'Thank you. Merry Christmas,' he responded. 'It don't seem like Christmas, somehow.'

'I'm not surprised. You haven't made a very good start with it, have you?'

Stephen shook his head dismally.

'What's more,' continued the old lady, 'you've put your poor foster parents, and me, to a mint of worry and trouble, by being such a wicked, thoughtless boy.'

'I'm sorry,' said the child. There was something perfunctory about the apology which roused Mrs Berry's ire.

'You *say* it,' she said explosively, 'but do you *mean* it? Do you realize that all this trouble stems from your selfishness? You've been given a good home, food, warmth, clothes, comfort, taken into a decent family, and how do you repay the Roses? You ask for something you know full well is too expensive for them to give you, and then you sulk because it's not forthcoming!'

The boy opened his mouth as though to protest against this harangue, but Mrs Berry swept on.

'You're a thoroughly nasty, mean-spirited little boy, eaten up with envy and jealousy, and if you don't fight against those things you're going to turn into a real criminal. You understand what I say?'

'Yes, but I never—'

'No excuses,' continued Mrs Berry briskly. 'You see what your sulking and envy led you to – breaking into my house and helping yourself to my Madeira cake. Those are crimes in themselves. If you were a few years older, you could be sent to prison for doing that.'

The child suddenly bent forward and put his head in his hands. She could see that he was fighting tears, and remained silent, watching him closely, and hoping that some of her words of wisdom had hit their mark.

'Have you ever had a spanking?' she asked suddenly.

'Only from me real mum. She gave me a clout now and again. The Roses don't hit none of us.'

'They're good people, better than you deserve, I suspect. I warrant if you'd been my little boy, you'd have had a few smacks by now, to show you the difference between right and wrong.'

There was a sniffing from the hidden face, but no comment. Mrs Berry's tone softened.

'What you've got to do, my child, is to start afresh. You've seen tonight where wickedness and self-pity lead you. For all we know, Mr and Mrs Rose are distracted – their Christmas spoiled – just because you must have your own way. And if they've told the police, then that's more people upset by your thoughtlessness.

'No, it's time you thought about other people instead of yourself. Time you counted your blessings, instead of making yourself miserable about things you covet. No selfish person is ever happy. Remember that.'

The boy nodded, and lifted his head from his hands. His cheeks were wet, and his expression was genuinely penitent.

'What we've got to do now,' said Mrs Berry, 'is to put things right as quickly and quietly as we can. Tell me, do you think the Roses will have missed you?'

The child looked bewildered.

'They don't never look in once they've tucked us up. They calls out, softlike, "Good night," when they goes to bed but don't open the door.'

'Not even on Christmas Eve?' asked Mrs Berry, broaching the subject delicately. Did the child still believe in Father Christmas? He had had enough to put up with this night, without any further painful disclosures.

'We has our presents on the breakfast table,' said Stephen, catching her meaning at once. 'And our stockings at teatime, when we light the candles on the Christmas tree.'

'So they may not know you left home?'

'I don't see how they can know till morning.'

'I see.'

Mrs Berry fell silent, turning over this fact in her mind. There seemed to be every hope that the child was right. If so, the sooner he returned, and crept back to bed, the better. It seemed proper in her straightforward mind, that having done wrong the boy himself should put it right.

She discounted the wrong done against herself and her own property, although she sincerely hoped that the child had learned his lesson. It was his attitude to his foster parents, and to all others with whom he must work and live, that must be altered.

'Do you go to church?' asked Mrs Berry.

'To Sunday school. Sometimes we go to Evensong.'

'Then you've heard about loving your neighbour.'

The child looked perplexed.

'Is it a commandment? We had to learn ten of those once, off of the church wall, at Sunday school.'

'It's another commandment: "Love they neighbour as thyself." Do you understand what it means?'

The child shook his head dumbly.

'Well, it sums up what I've been telling you. Think about other people and their feelings. Consider them as much as you consider yourself. Put yourself in your foster parents' place, for instance. How would you feel if the boy you looked after was so discontented that he ran away, making you feel that you had let him down, when all the time you had been doing your level best to make him happy?'

The boy looked at his hands, and said nothing.

'You're going to go back, Stephen, and get into that house as quietly as you can, and get into bed. Can you do it?'

'Of course. The larder window's never shut. I've been in and out dozens of times.'

'And you say nothing at all about what has happened tonight. It's a secret between you and me. Understand?'

'Yes,' he whispered.

'There's no need for anyone to be upset by this, except

you. I hope you'll have learned your lesson well enough to be cheerful and grateful for all that you are given, and all that's done for you, on Christmas Day. Do you promise that?'

The boy nodded. Then his eyes grew round, as he looked at Mrs Berry in alarm.

'But s'pose they've found out?'

'I was coming to that,' said the old lady calmly. 'You tell them the truth, make a clean breast of it, and say you'll never do it again – and mean it, what's more!'

The child's eyes grew terrified. 'Tell them about coming in here?'

'Of course. And tell them I should like to see them, to explain matters.'

'And the police?'

'If the police have been troubled, then you apologize to them too. You know what I told you. You must face the consequences whatever they are. This night should make you think in future, my boy, and a very good thing too.'

She stood up, and moved to the window. Outside, the rain had stopped, but a stiff wind blew the ragged clouds swiftly across a watery moon, and ruffled the surface of the puddles.

It was a good step to Tupps Hill, but Stephen must be on his way shortly. Mrs Berry was not blind to the dangers of the night for a young child walking the lanes alone, but it was a risk that had to be taken. At least the weather was kinder, the child's clothing was dry, and he had eaten and slept. He had got himself into this situation, and it would do him no harm, thought Mrs Berry sturdily, to get himself out of it. In any case, the chance of meeting anyone abroad at half-past three on Christmas morning was remote.

'Put your clothes on,' directed the old lady, 'while I make us both a cup of coffee.'

She left him struggling with the toggle fastenings as she went into the kitchen. When she returned with the steaming cups of coffee, the boy was lacing his shoes. He looked up, smiling. He was so like Pepe, in that fleeting moment, that the years vanished for old Mrs Berry.

'Lovely and warm,' Stephen said approvingly, holding up his feet.

Mrs Berry handed him his cup, and offered the biscuit tin. As he nibbled his Ginger Nut with his prominent front teeth, Stephen's resemblance to a mouse was more marked than ever.

The old lady shuddered. Was her own little horror, the mouse, still at large above? Mrs Berry craved for her bed. She was suddenly stiff and bone-tired, and longed for oblivion. What a night it had been! Would the boy ever remember anything that she had tried to teach him? She had her doubts, but one could only try. Who knows? Something might stick in that scatterbrained head.

She motioned to the child to fetch his coat, turned the sleeves the right way out, and helped to button it to the neck. His chin was smooth and warm against her wrinkled hand, and reminded her with sudden poignancy of her own sleeping grandchildren.

She held him by the lapels of his raincoat, and looked searchingly into his dark eyes.

'You remember the promise? Say nothing, if they know nothing. Speak the truth if they do. And in future, do what's right and not what's wrong.'

The child nodded solemnly.

She kissed him on the cheek, gently and without smiling. They went to the front door together, Mrs Berry lifting a bar of chocolate from the Christmas tree as she passed.

'Put it in your pocket. You've a long way to go and may get hungry. Straight home, mind, and into bed. Promise?'

'Promise.'

She opened the door quietly. It was fairly light, the moon partially visible through fast-scudding clouds. The wind lifted her hair and rustled dead leaves in the road.

'Good-bye then, Stephen. Don't forget what I've told you,' she whispered.

'Good-bye,' he whispered back.

He stood motionless for a second, as if wondering how to make his farewell, then turned suddenly and began the long trudge home.

Mrs Berry watched him go, waiting for him to turn, perhaps, and wave. But the child did not look back, and she watched him walking steadily – left, right, left, right – until the bend in the lane hid him from her sight.

CHAPTER NINE

Back in the warm living room Mrs Berry found herself swaying on her feet with exhaustion. She steadied herself by holding on to the back of the armchair that had been her refuge for the night.

It was years since she had felt such utter tiredness. It reminded her of the days when, as a young girl, she had helped with the mounds of washing at the vicarage. She had spent an hour or more at a time turning the heavy mangle – a monster of cast iron and solid wood – in the steamy atmosphere of the washhouse.

She looked now at her downy nest of feather pillow and eiderdown, and knew that if she sat down sleep would engulf her. She would be stiff when she awoke for every nerve and sinew in her old body craved for the comfort of her bed, with room to stretch her heavy limbs.

She would brave that dratted mouse! Ten chances to one it had made its way home again, and, in any case, she was so tired she would see and hear nothing once she was abed.

She glanced round the room. The fire must be raked through, and the two telltale coffee cups washed and put away. Mrs Berry had no intention of telling Mary and the little girls about her visitor.

She put all to rights, moving slowly, her limbs leaden, her eyes half-closed with fatigue. She drew back the curtains, ready for the daylight, and scanned the stormy sky.

The moon was high now. Ragged clouds skimmed across its face, so that the glimpses of the wet trees and shining road were intermittent. The boy should be well on his way by now. She hoped that he had avoided the great puddles that silvered his path. Those shoes would be useless in this weather.

The old lady sighed, and turned back to the armchair, folding the eiderdown neatly and putting the plump pillow across it. Gathering up her bundle, she took one last look at the scene of her encounter with young Stephen. Then, shouldering her burden, she opened the door to the staircase and went, very slowly, to her bedroom.

Exhaustion dulled the terror that stirred her at the thought of the mouse still at large. Nevertheless, the old lady's heart beat faster as she quietly opened the bedroom door. The great double bed was as welcome a sight as a snug harbour to a storm-battered boat.

Mary had turned down the bedclothes. They gleamed, smooth and white as a snowdrift, in the faint light of the moon.

The room was still and cool after the living room. Mrs Berry stood motionless, listening for any scuffle or scratching that might betray her enemy. But all was silent.

She switched on the bedside lamp, which had been Mary's last year's Christmas present. It had a deep-pink shade that sent a rosy glow into the room. The old lady replaced her pillow and spread out the eiderdown, then, nerving herself, she bent down stiffly to look under the bed and see if the intruder was still there.

All was as it should be. She scanned the rest of the

floor, and saw the mousetrap. It was empty, and the second piece of cheese was still untouched.

Mrs Berry's spirits rose a little. Surely, this might mean that the mouse had returned to his own home? He would either have been caught, or the cheese would have been eaten, as before. But the trap must not be left there, a danger to the grandchildren, who would come running in barefoot, all too soon, to show their tired grandmother the things that Father Christmas had brought.

Mrs Berry took a shoe from the floor and tapped the trap smartly. The crack of the spring snapping made her jump but now all was safe. She could not bring herself to touch the horrid thing with her bare fingers, but prodded it to safety, under the dressing table, with her shoe.

Sighing with relief, the old lady climbed into bed, drew up the bedclothes and stretched luxuriously.

How soon, she wondered, before Stephen Amonetti would be enjoying his bed, as she did now?

At the rate he was stepping out, thought Mrs Berry drowsily, he must be descending the long slope that led to the fold in the downs at the foot of Tupps Hill.

She knew that road well. The meadows on that southern slope had been full of cowslips when little Amelia Scott and her friends were children. She could smell them now, warm and sweet in the May sunshine. She loved the way the pale green stalks grew from the flat rosettes of leaves, so like living pen wipers, soft and fleshy, half hidden in the springy grass of the downland.

The children made cowslip balls as well as bunches to carry home. Some of the mothers made cowslip wine, and secretly young Amelia grieved to see the beautiful flowers torn from their stalks and tossed hugger-mugger into a

basket. They were too precious for such rough treatment, the child felt, though she relished a sip of the wine when it was made, and now tasted it again on her tongue, the very essence of a sunny May day.

On those same slopes, in wintertime, she had tobogganed with those same friends. She remembered a childhood sweetheart, a black-haired charmer called Ned, who always led the way on his homemade sled and feared nothing. He scorned gloves, hats, and all the other winter comforts in which loving mothers wrapped their offspring, but rushed bareheaded down the slope, his eyes sparkling, cheeks red, and the breath blowing behind him in streamers.

Poor Ned, so full of life and courage! He had gone to a

water-filled grave in Flanders' mud before he was twenty years old. But the memory of that vivacious child remained with old Mrs Berry as freshly as if it were yesterday that they had swept down the snowy slope together.

In those days a tumbledown shack had stood by a small rivulet at the bottom of the slope. It was inhabited by a poor, silly, old man, called locally Dirty Dick. He did not seem to have any steady occupation, although he sometimes did a little field work in the summer months, singling turnips, picking the wild oats from the farmers' standing corn, or making himself useful when the time came round for picking apples or plums in the local orchards.

The children were warned not to speak to him. Years before, it seemed, he had been taken to court in Caxley for some indecent conduct, and this was never forgotten. The rougher children shouted names after him and threw stones. The more gently nurtured, such as little Amelia, simply hurried by.

'You're not to take any notice of him,' her mother had said warningly.

'Why not?'

A look of the utmost primness swept over her mother's countenance.

'He is sometimes a very *rude* old man,' she said, in a shocked voice.

Amelia enquired no further.

His end had been tragic, she remembered. He had been found, face downwards, in the little brook, a saucepan in his clenched hand as he had dipped for water to boil for his morning tea. The doctor had said his heart must have failed suddenly. The old man had toppled into the stream and drowned in less than eight inches of spring flood water.

Young Amelia had heard of his death with mingled horror and relief. Now she need never fear to pass that hut, dreading the meeting with 'a very *rude* old man', whose death, nevertheless, seemed unnecessarily cruel to the soft-hearted child.

Well, Stephen Amonetti would have no Dirty Dick to fear on his homeward way, but he would have the avenue to traverse, a frightening tunnel of dark trees lining the road for a matter of a hundred yards across the valley. Even on the hottest day, the air blew chill in those deep shadows. On a night like this, Mrs Berry knew well, the wind would clatter the branches and whistle eerily. Stephen would need to keep a stout heart to hold the bogies at bay as he ran the gauntlet to those age-old trees.

But by then he would be within half a mile of his home, up the steep short hill that overlooked the valley. A small estate of council houses had been built at Tupps Hill, some thirty years ago, and thought the architecture was grimly functional and the concrete paths gave an institutional look to the area, yet most of the tenants – countrymen all – had softened the bleakness with climbing wall plants and plenty of bright annuals in the borders.

The hillside position, too, was enviable. The houses commanded wide views over agricultural land, the gardens were large and, with unusual forethought, the council had provided a row of garages for their tenants, so that unsightly, old shabby cars were screened from view. Those lucky enough to get a Tupps Hill house were envied by their brethren.

If only Stephen could get in unobserved! Mrs Berry stirred restlessly, considering her visitor's chances of escaping detection. Poor little mouse! Poor little Christmas mouse! Dear God, please let him creep into his home safely!

And then she froze. Somewhere, in the darkness close at hand, something rustled.

Her first instinct was to snatch the eiderdown from the bed, and bolt. She would fly downstairs again to the safety of the armchair, and there await the dawn and Mary's coming to her rescue.

But several things kept her quaking in the warm bed. Extreme tiredness was one. Her fear that she would rouse the sleeping household was another. The day ahead would be a busy one, and Mary needed all the rest she could get. This was something she must face alone.

Mrs Berry tried to pinpoint the position of the rustling. A faint squeaking noise made her flesh prickle. What could it be? It did not sound like the squeak of a mouse. The noise came from the right, by the window. Could the wretched creature be on the windowsill? Could it be scrabbling, with its tiny claws, on the glass of the windowpane, in its efforts to escape?

Mrs Berry shuddered at the very thought of confronting it, of seeing its dreadful stringy tail, its beady eyes, and its more than likely darting to cover into some inaccessible spot in the bedroom.

All her old terrors came flying back, like a flock of evil black birds, to harass her. There was that ghastly dead mouse in her aunt's flour keg, the next one with all those pink hairless babies in her father's toolbox, the one that the boys killed in the school lobby, the pair that set up home once under the kitchen sink, and all those numberless little horrors that Pepe the cat used to bring in, alive and dead, to scare her out of her wits.

But somehow, there had always been someone to cope with them. Dear Stanley, or Bertie, or brave Mary, or some good neighbour would come to her aid. Now, in the darkness, she must manage alone.

She took a deep breath and cautiously edged her tired old legs out of the bed. She must switch on the bedside lamp again, and risk the fact that it might stampede the mouse into flight.

Her fingers shook as she groped for the switch. Once more, rosy light bathed the room. Sitting on the side of the bed, Mrs Berry turned round to face the direction of the rustling, fear drying her throat.

There was no sound now. Even the wind seemed to have dropped. Silence engulfed the room. Could she have been mistaken? Could the squeaking noise have been caused by the thorns of the rosebush growing against the wall? Hope rose. Immediately it fell again.

For there, crouched in a corner of the windowsill, was a tiny furry ball.

Old Mrs Berry put a shaking hand over her mouth to quell any scream that might escape her unawares. Motionless, she gazed at the mouse. Motionless, the mouse gazed back. Thus transfixed, they remained. Only the old lady's heavy breathing broke the silence that engulfed them.

After some minutes, the mouse lifted its head and

snuffed the air. Mrs Berry caught her breath. It was so like Stephen Amonetti, as he had sprawled in the armchair, head back, with his pointed pink nose in the air. She watched the mouse, fascinated. It seemed oblivious of danger and sat up on its haunches to wash its face.

Its bright eyes, as dark and lustrous as Stephen's, moved restlessly as it went about its toilet. Its minute pink paws reminded Mrs Berry of the tiny pink shells she had treasured as a child after a Sunday-school outing to the sea. It was incredible to think that something so small could lead such a full busy life, foraging, making a home, keeping itself and its family fed and cleaned.

And that was the life it must return to, thought Mrs Berry firmly. It must go back, as surely as Stephen had, to resume its proper existence. Strange that two creatures, so alike in looks, should flee their homes and take refuge on the same night, uninvited, under her roof!

The best way to send this little scrap on its homeward journey would be to open the window and hope that it would negotiate the frail stairway of the rosebush trained against the wall, and so return to earth. But the thought of reaching over the mouse to struggle with the window catch needed all the courage that the old lady could muster, and she sat on the bed summoning her strength.

The longer she watched, the less frightened she became. It was almost like watching Stephen Amonetti all over again – a fugitive, defenceless, young, and infinitely pathetic. They both needed help and guidance to get them home.

She took a deep breath and stood up. The bed springs squeaked, but the mouse did not take flight. It stopped washing its whiskers and gazed warily about it. Mrs Berry, gritting her teeth, approached slowly.

The mouse shrank down into a little furry ball, reminding Mrs Berry of a fur button on a jacket of her mother's. Quietly, she leaned over the sill and lifted the window catch. The mouse remained motionless.

The cold air blew in, stirring the curtain and bringing a breath of rain-washed leaves and damp earth.

Mrs Berry retreated to the bed again to watch developments. She sat there for a full minute before her captive made a move.

It raised its quivering pink nose and then, in one bound, darted over the window frame, dragging its pink tail behind it. As it vanished, Mrs Berry hurried to the window to watch its departure.

It was light enough to see its tiny shape undulating down the crisscross of thorny rose stems. But when it finally reached the bare earth, it was invisible to the old lady's eyes.

She closed the window carefully, sighed with relief and exhaustion, and clambered, once more, into bed.

Her two unbidden visitors – her Christmas mice – had gone! Now, at long last, she could rest.

Behind the row of wallflower plants, close to the bricks of the cottage, scurried the mouse, nose twitching. It ran across the garden path, dived under the cotoneaster bush, scrambled up the mossy step by the disused well, turned sharp right through the jungle of dried grass beside the garden shed, and streaked, unerringly, to the third hawthorn bush in the hedge.

There, at the foot, screened by ground ivy, was its hole.

It dived down into the loose sandy earth, snuffling the dear frowsty smell of mouse family and mouse food.

Home at last!

At much the same time, Stephen Amonetti lowered himself carefully through the pantry window.

The house was as silent as the grave, and dark inside, after the pallid glimmer of the moon's rays.

With infinite caution he undid the pantry door, and closed it behind him. For greater quietness, he removed his wet shoes and, carrying them in one hand, he ascended the staircase.

The smells of home were all about him. There was a faint whiff of the mince pies Mrs Rose had made on Christmas Eve mingled, from the open door of the bathroom, with the sharp clean smell of Lifebuoy soap.

Noiselessly, he turned the handle of the bedroom door. Now there was a stronger scent – of the liniment that Jim used after football, boasting, as he rubbed, of his swelling muscles. The older boy lay curled on his side of the bed, dead to the world. It would take more than Stephen's entry into the room to wake him.

Peeling off his clothes, Stephen longed for bed, for sleep, for forgetfulness. Within three minutes, he was lying beside the sleeping boy, his head a jumble of cake tins, fierce old ladies, stormy weather, sore feet.

And somewhere, beyond the muddle, a hazy remembrance of a promise to keep.

Chapter Ten

It was light when Mrs Berry awoke. She lay inert in the warm bed, relishing its comfort, as her bemused mind struggled with memories of the night.

The mouse and Stephen! What a double visitation, to be sure! No wonder she was tired this morning and had slept late. It must be almost eight o'clock – Christmas morning too! Where were the children? Where was Mary? The house was uncommonly quiet. She must get up and investigate.

At that moment, she heard footsteps outside in the road, and the sound of people greeting each other. Simultaneously, the church bell began to ring. Yes, it must be nearly eight o'clock, and those good parishioners were off to early service!

Well, thought Mrs Berry philosophically, she would not be among the congregation. She rarely missed the eight o'clock service, but after such a night she would be thankful to go later, at eleven, taking the two little girls with her.

She struggled up in bed and gazed at the sky. It was a glory of grey and gold: streamers of ragged clouds, gilded at their edges, filled the world with a luminous radiance, against which the bare twigs of the plum tree spread their black lace.

She opened the window, remembering with a shudder the last time she had done so. Now the air, fresh and cool, lifted her hair. The bells sounded clearly, as the neighbours' footsteps died away into the distance.

'Awake then?' said Mary, opening the door. 'Happy Christmas!'

She bore a cup of tea, the steam blowing towards her in the draught from the window.

'You spoil me,' said Mrs Berry. 'I ought to be up. Proper old sleepyhead I am today. Where are the children?'

'Downstairs, having breakfast. Not that they want much. They've been stuffing sweets and the tangerine from their stockings since six!'

She put the cup on the bedside table and closed the window.

'They wanted to burst in here, but I persuaded them to let you sleep on. What happened to the mouse? Is it still about? I see the trap's sprung.'

'I let it out of the window,' said Mrs Berry. She could not keep a touch of pride from her voice.

'You never! You brave old dear! Where was it then?'

'On the sill. I got so tired by about three, I risked it and came up. I don't mind admitting I fair hated reaching over the little creature to get at the latch, but it made off in no time, so that was all right.'

'That took some pluck,' said Mary, her voice warm with admiration. 'Can I let those rascals come up now, to show you their presents?'

'Yes, please,' said Mrs Berry, reaching for her cup. 'Then I'll get up, and give you a hand.'

Mary called down the staircase, and there was a thumping of feet and squeals and shouts as the two excited children struggled upstairs with their loot.

'Look, Grandma,' shouted Frances, 'I've put on my slippers!'

'Look, Grandma,' shouted Jane, 'Father Christmas brought me a dear little doll!'

They flung themselves upon the bed, Mary watching them with amusement.

'Mind Gran's tea,' she warned.

'Leave them be,' said her mother lovingly. 'This is how Christmas morning should begin!'

Smiling, Mary left the three of them and went downstairs.

On the door mat lay an envelope. Mary's heart sank, as she bent to pick it up. Not another person they'd forgotten to send to? Not another case of Mrs Burton all over again? Anyway, it was too late now to run about returning Christmas cards. Whoever had sent it must just be thanked when they met.

She took it into the living room and stood with her back to the fire, studying the face of the envelope with some bewilderment. Most of the cards were addressed to 'Mrs Berry and Family,' or to 'Mrs Berry and Mrs Fuller,' but this was to 'Mrs Bertie Fuller' alone, and written in a firm hand.

Wonderingly, Mary drew out the card. It was a fine reproduction of 'The Nativity' by G. van Honthorst, and inside, beneath the printed Christmas greetings, was the signature of Ray Bullen. A small piece of writing paper fluttered to the floor, as Mary, flushing with pleasure, studied the card.

She stooped to retrieve it. The message it contained was simple and to the point.

I have two tickets for the New Year's Eve concert at the
Corn Exchange. Can you come with me? Do hope so!

RAY

Mary sat down with a thud on the chair recently
vacated by young Jane. Automatically, she began stacking the girls' bowls sticky with cornflakes and milk. Her
hands were shaking, she noticed, and she felt shame
mingling with her happiness.

'Like some stupid girl,' she scolded herself, 'instead of a
widow with two girls.'

She left the crockery alone, and took up the note again.
It was kind of him – typical of his thoughtfulness. Somehow, he had managed to write the card after seeing her
yesterday, and had found someone in the village who
would drop it through her letterbox on the way to early
service. It must have taken some organizing, thought
Mary, much touched. He was a good sort of man. Bertie
had always said so, and this proved it.

As for the invitation, that was a wonderful thing to
have. She would love to go and knew that her mother
would willingly look after the children. But would she
approve? Would she think she was being disloyal to
Bertie's memory to accept an invitation from another
man?

Fiddlesticks! thought Mary robustly, dismissing such
mawkish sentiments. Here was an old friend offering to
take her to a concert – that was all. It was a kindness that
would be churlish to rebuff. Of course she would go, and
it would be a rare treat too!

Calmer, she rose and began to take the dishes into the
kitchen, her mind fluttering about the age-old problem of

what to wear on such a momentous occasion. There was her black, but it was too funereal, too widowlike. Suddenly she wanted to look gay, young, happy – to show that she appreciated the invitation, she told herself hastily.

There was the yellow frock she had bought impulsively one summer day, excusing her extravagance by persuading herself that it was just the thing for the Women's Institute outing to the theatre. But when the evening had arrived she had begun to have doubts. Was it, perhaps, too gay for a widow? Would the tongues wag? Would they say she was 'after' someone? Mutton dressed as lamb?

She had put it back in the cupboard, and dressed herself in the black one. Better be on the safe side, she had told herself dejectedly, and had felt miserable the whole evening.

Yes, the yellow frock should have an airing, and her bronze evening shoes an extra shine. Ray Bullen should have no cause to regret his invitation.

She turned on the tap, as the children came rushing into the room.

'Why, Mummy,' exclaimed Frances, wide eyed with amazement, *'you're singing!'*

Upstairs Mrs Berry put on her grey woollen jumper and straightened the Welsh tweed skirt. This was her working outfit. Later in the morning she would change into more elegant attire, suitable for church-going, but there was housework to be done in the next hour or two. Last of all, she tied a blue and white spotted apron round her waist, and was ready to face the day.

Once more, she opened the window. The small birds chirped and chatted below, awaiting their morning crumbs. A grey and white wagtail teetered back and forth across a puddle, looking for all the world like a miniature curate, with his white collar and dove-grey garments. The yellow winter jasmine starred the wall below, forerunner of the aconites and snowdrops soon to come. There was a hopeful feeling of spring in the air, decided Mrs Berry, gazing at the sky. How different from yesterday's gloom!

The children's happiness was infectious. Their delight in the simple presents warmed the old lady's heart and set her thinking of that other child, less fortunate, who had no real family of his own and who had wept because of it.

How was he faring? Had he, after all, found a watch among his parcels? Mrs Berry doubted it. The Roses had spoken truly when they told the child that a watch was too much to expect at Christmas. No doubt, lesser presents would make him happy, assuaging to some extent that fierce longing to have a watch like Patsy's and Jim's. A passionate child, thought Mrs Berry, shaking her head sadly. Pepe all over again! It made life hard for the boy, and harder still for those who had to look after him. Would he ever remember any of the good advice she had tried to offer? Knowing the ways of children, she suspected that most of her admonitions had gone in one ear and out of the other.

Ah well! One could only hope, she thought, descending the staircase.

Mary had set a tray at the end of the table for her mother. Beyond it stood the pink cyclamen and a pile of parcels.

The two children, hopping from leg to leg with excitement, hovered on each side of the chair.

'Come on, Gran! Come and see what you've got. Mum gave you the plant!'

'Mary,' exclaimed Mrs Berry, hands in the air with astonishment, 'you shouldn't have spent so much money on me! What a beauty! And so many buds to come out too. Well, I don't know when I've seen a finer cyclamen, and that's a fact.'

She kissed her daughter warmly. Why, the girl seemed aglow! Christmas was a comforting time, for old and young, thought Mrs Berry, reaching out for the parcels.

'Open mine first,' demanded Frances.

'No, mine,' said Jane. 'I'm the oldest.'

'I'll open them together,' said the old lady, taking one in each hand. 'See, I'll tear this bit off this one, then this bit off that one—'

She tugged at the wrappings gently.

'No, no!' cried Jane, unable to bear the delay. 'Do one first – don't matter which – then the other. But read the tags. We wrote 'em ourselves.'

Mrs Berry held the two tags at arm's length. Her spectacles were mislaid amidst the Christmas debris.

' "Darling Grandma, with love from Jane," ' she read aloud. She shook the parcel, then smelled it, then held it to her ear. The children hugged each other in rapture.

'Why do you listen to it?' queried Frances. 'Do you think there's a bird in it?'

'A watch perhaps,' said Mrs Berry, surprised by her own words.

'A *watch*?' screamed the girls. 'But you've got a watch!'

'So I have,' said Mrs Berry calmly. 'Well, let's see what's in here.'

Wrapped in four thicknesses of tissue paper was a little egg-timer.

'Now, *that*,' cried the old lady, 'is *exactly* what I wanted. Clever Jane!'

She kissed the child's soft cheek.

'Now mine!' begged Frances. 'Quick! Undo it *quick*, Gran.'

'I must read the tag. "Dear Gran, Happy Christmas, Frances." Very nice.'

'*Undo it!*' said the child.

Obediently, the old lady undid the paper. Inside was a box of peppermint creams.

'My favourite sweets!' said Mrs Berry. 'What a kind child you are! Would you like one now?'

'Yes please,' both said in unison.

'I hoped you'd give us one,' said Frances, beaming. 'Isn't it lucky we like them too?'

'Very lucky,' agreed their grandmother, proffering the box.

'Let Gran have her breakfast, do,' Mary said, appearing from the kitchen.

'But she's got lots more parcels to open!'

'I shall have a cup of tea first,' said the old lady, 'and then undo them.'

Sighing at such maddening adult behaviour, the two children retired to the other end of the table where they had set out a tiny metal tea set of willow pattern in blue and white.

'This is my favourite present,' announced Frances, 'and the teapot pours. See?'

Mary and her mother exchanged amused glances. The set had been one of several small toys they had bought together in Caxley to fill up the stockings. The chief present for each girl had been a doll, beautifully dressed in handmade clothes worked on secretly when the girls were in bed. It was typical of children the world over that some trifle of no real value should give them more immediate pleasure than the larger gifts.

At last, all the presents were unwrapped. Bath cubes, stockings, handkerchiefs, sweets, a tin of biscuits, another of tea, and a tablecloth embroidered by Mary – all were displayed and admired. Mary's presents had to be brought from the sideboard and shown to her mother, to please the two children, despite the fact that Mrs Berry had seen most of them before.

'Now, what's to do in the kitchen?' asked Mrs Berry, rising from the table.

'Nothing. The pudding's in, and the bird is ready, and the vegetables.'

'Then I'll dust and tidy up,' declared Mrs Berry. 'Upstairs first. I can guess what the girls' room looks like!'

'At least there are no mice!' laughed Mary.

The children looked up, alert.

'No mice? Was there a mouse? Where is it now?'

Their grandmother told them about the intruder, and how she had settled by the fire, but at last gone up to bed and had let the mouse out of the window.

What would they have said, she wondered, as she told her tale, if she had told them the whole story? How their eyes would have widened at the thought of a boy – a *big* boy of nine – breaking into their home and trying to steal their grandmother's Madeira cake! As it was, the story of the real mouse stirred their imagination.

'I expect it was hungry,' said Jane with pity. 'I expect it smelled all the nice Christmas food and came in to have a little bit.'

'It had plenty of its own sort of food outdoors,' Mrs Berry retorted tartly.

'Perhaps it just wanted to see inside a house,' suggested Frances reasonably. 'You shouldn't have frightened it away, Gran.'

'It frightened *me* away,' said the old lady.

'Perhaps it will come back,' said Jane hopefully.

'That,' said her grandmother forcefully, 'I sincerely hope it will not do.'

And she went upstairs to her duties.

When the children and her mother had departed to church, the house was blessedly quiet. Mary, basting the turkey and turning potatoes in the baking dish, had time to ponder her invitation. As soon as the children were safely out of the way she would have a word with her mother, then reply.

But where should she send it? There had been no address on the note, and although she knew the part of Caxley in which Ray lived, she could not recall the name of the road, and certainly had no idea of the number. Perhaps the best thing would be to send it to the office of *The Caxley Chronicle*, where he worked. He would be going into work, no doubt, on the day after Boxing Day. Plenty of time to spare before New Year's Eve.

Now that the first initial surprise of the invitation was over, Mary found herself growing more and more delighted at the thought of the evening outing. Caxley had produced a New Year's Eve concert as long as she could remember, and she and Bertie had attended several of them.

The Corn Exchange was always full. It was something of an occasion. The mayor came, all the local gentry sat in the front rows, and everyone knew that the music provided would be good rousing stuff by Handel and Bach and Mozart, with maybe a light sprinkling of Gilbert and Sullivan, or Edward German, or Lionel Monckton, as a garnish.

It was definitely a social affair, when one wore one's best, and hoped to see one's friends and be seen by them. It would be good, thought Mary, to have a personable man as an escort instead of attending a function on her own.

Kind Ray! Good Quaker Ray! How did that passage go in the library book – 'Very thoughtful and wealthy and good'? She could vouch for two of those virtues anyway!

She slammed the oven door shut and laughed aloud.

At one o'clock the Christmas dinner – everything done to a turn – was set upon the table, and the two little girls attacked their plates with enviable appetite. Their elders ate more circumspectly.

Nevertheless, at two o'clock it was the children who played energetically on the floor with their new toys, whilst Mary and her mother lay back in their armchairs and succumbed to that torpor induced by unaccustomed rich food.

'We must take a turn in the fresh air before it

gets dark.' Mrs Berry yawned; Mary nodded agreement drowsily.

They woke at three, much refreshed, donned their coats and gloves, and set off. The bright clouds of morning had gone; a gentle grey light veiled the distant scene.

The four of them walked towards the slope where young Stephen had walked scarcely twelve hours earlier. Mrs Berry's mind was full of memories of her Christmas visitor. She strode along, dwelling on the oddity of events that had brought one of the Amonetti family into her life once more.

Ahead of her, holding a child by each hand, Mary was running a few steps, then stopping suddenly to bring the two children face to face in an ecstatic embrace. It was a game they had loved as toddlers, but it was years, thought Mrs Berry, since Mary had played it with them.

Their delighted screams matched the calling of the flight of rooks above, slowly winging homewards against the evening sky.

Now they had reached the top of the slope, and Mary, breathless, stopped to wait for her mother.

They stood together looking across the shallow valley, already filling with the pale mist of winter.

'That's Tupps Hill over there, isn't it?' said Mary.

Her mother nodded. 'D'you remember the Roses?'

'Vaguely,' said Mary. 'Why?'

There was an intensity about her mother's gaze that made Mary curious.

The old lady did not answer for a moment, her eyes remained fixed upon the shadowy hill beyond the rising mist.

'I might call on them one day,' she said, at last. 'Not yet awhile. But some day – some day, perhaps.' She turned suddenly. 'Let's get home, Mary dear. There's no place like it – and it's getting cold.'

CHAPTER ELEVEN

It was hardly surprising at teatime, to find that the family's appetite was small, despite the afternoon walk.

'I'll just bring in the Christmas cake,' said Mary, 'and the tea tray. Though I expect you'd like a slice of your Madeira, wouldn't you?'

'No, thank you,' replied Mrs Berry hastily.

She pondered on the fate of the Madeira cake as Mary clattered china in the kitchen. It certainly seemed a terrible waste of sugar and butter and eggs, not to mention the beautiful curl of angelica that cost dear knows how much these days. But there it was. The thought of those pink paws touching it was enough to put anyone off the food.

Perhaps she could cut off the outside, and slice the rest for a trifle? Waste was something that Mrs Berry abhorred. But at once she dismissed the idea. It was no good. The cake must go. No doubt the birds would relish it, but she must find an opportunity for disposing of it when Mary was absent from the scene. Explanations would be difficult, under the circumstances.

Mary returned with the tray. To the accompaniment of cries of appreciation from the children the candles were lighted on the Christmas tree and at each end of the mantelpiece.

Outside, the early dusk had fallen, and the shadowy room, lit by a score of flickering candle flames and the glow from the fire, had never looked so snug and magical, thought Mrs Berry. If only their menfolk could have been with them . . .

She shook away melancholy as she had done so often. The time for grieving was over. There was much to be thankful for. She looked at Mary, intent upon cutting the snowy cake, and the rosy children, their eyes reflecting the light from the candles, and she was content.

And that child at Tupps Hill? Was he as happy as her own? She had a feeling that he might be – that perhaps he had been able to let the Christmas spirit soothe his anxious heart.

Jane's Christmas cracker had yielded a tiny spinning top that had numbers printed on it. When it came to rest,

after being twirled on the table, the number that was uppermost gave the spinner his score. This simple toy provided part of the evening's play time, and all four played.

Later, Mrs Berry played Ludo with the children – a new game found in Frances' pillow slip – while Mary wrote some thank-you letters. By seven o'clock both children were yawning, although they did their best to hide this weakness from the grown-ups. It would be terrible to miss anything on this finest day of the year.

'Bed,' said Mary firmly, and as the wails greeted her dictum, she relented enough to say: 'You can take your toys upstairs and play with them for a little while.'

Within half an hour, they were safely in bed, and Mary and her mother sat down to enjoy the respite from the children's clamour.

'Why, there's a new Christmas card!' exclaimed Mrs Berry, her eye lighting on Mary's from Ray.

Mary rose to fetch it from the mantelpiece and handed it to her mother.

'Someone dropped it through the letterbox first thing this morning. I bumped into Ray yesterday when we were shopping and he helped us on to the bus with our parcels.'

'Typical of the Bullens,' commented Mrs Berry, studying the card with approval. 'I knew his mother when she was young. A nice girl.'

Mary took a breath. This seemed as propitious a time as any other to mention the invitation.

'There is a note somewhere. He has asked me to go to the New Year's Eve concert. Would you mind? Looking after the girls, I mean?'

'Good heavens, no! I'm glad to think of you getting out a little. You'll enjoy an evening with Ray Bullen,' said her mother easily.

Mrs Berry leaned back in the chair and closed her eyes. It had been a long day, and she was near to sleep. A jumble of impressions, bright fragments of the last twenty-four hours, jostled together in her tired mind like the tiny pieces of coloured glass in a child's kaleidoscope.

Stephen's mousey face, his pink hand spread like a starfish upon his knee, with a shining tear upon it. Her own shadow, poker in hand, monstrously large on the passage wall as she approached the unknown intruder. The furry scrap crouched on the windowsill with the wild weather beyond. Stephen's resolute back, vanishing round the bend of the lane as he marched home. The reflection of the candles in her grandchildren's eyes. The candles in the church – dozens of them today – and the sweet clear voices of the choir boys.

She woke with a jerk. The clock showed that she had slept for ten minutes. Her last impression still filled her mind.

'It was lovely in church this morning,' she said to Mary. 'Flowers and candles, and the boys singing so sweetly. You should have come.'

'I will next Sunday,' Mary promised. 'A New Year's resolution, Mum.'

There was a quiet happiness about Mary that did not escape Mrs Berry's eyes, but in her wisdom she said nothing.

Things, she knew in her bones, were falling, delicately and rightly, into place.

'I'll go and tuck up the girls,' said Mrs Berry, struggling from her chair, 'and switch off their light.'

She mounted the stairs and was surprised to see that both children were in her own room. They were kneeling on her bed, very busy with something on the window-sill.

They turned at her approach.

'We're just putting out a little supper for the Christmas mouse,' explained Jane.

On the ledge was one of the doll's tin willow pattern plates. Upon it were a few crumbs of Christmas cake and one or two holly berries.

'They're apples for him,' said Frances. 'When people call you should always offer them refreshment, Mummy says.'

Mrs Berry remembered the steaming bowl of bread and milk clutched against a duffel coat.

'She's quite right,' she said, smiling at them. 'But somehow I don't think that mouse will come back.'

Stephen's dwindling figure, striding away, came before her eyes. The children looked at her, suddenly forlorn. She offered swift comfort.

'But I'm sure of one thing. That Christmas mouse will remember his visit here for the rest of his life.'

The rising moon silvered the roofs at Shepherds Cross and turned the puddles into mirrors. The sky was cloudless. Soon the frost would come, furring the grass and hedges, glazing the cattle troughs and water butts.

Dick Rose, at Tupps Hill, was glad to get back to the fireside after shutting up the hens for the night.

The table had been pushed back against the wall, and the

three children were crawling about the floor, engrossed in a clockwork train that rattled merrily around a maze of lines set all over the floor. Betty sat watching them, as delighted as they were with its bustling manoeuvres.

'It's only fell off once,' said Stephen proudly, looking up at his foster father's entrance.

'Good,' said Dick. He never wasted words.

'Are you sad Father Christmas never brought you a watch?' asked Patsy of Stephen.

Dick's eyes met his wife's. Patsy was still young enough to believe in the myth, and the boys had nobly resisted enlightening her.

Stephen turned dark eyes upon her.

'Never thought about it,' he lied bravely. 'I've got all this, haven't I?'

He picked up the little train, and held it, whirring, close to his face. He turned and smiled – the radiant warm smile of his lost father – upon his foster parents.

'You're a good kid,' said Dick gruffly. 'And your birthday ain't far off.'

For the first time since Stephen's tempestuous arrival, he thought suddenly, the boy seemed part of the family.

There was a stirring beneath the third bush in the hawthorn hedge. A sharp nose pushed aside the ground-ivy leaves, and the mouse emerged into the moonlight.

It paused, sniffing the chill air, then ran through the dry grass by the shed, negotiated the mossy step by the wellhead, and stopped to nibble a dried seed pod.

On it ran again, parting the crisp grass with its sinuous body, diving down ruts, scrambling up slopes, until it gained the wet earth behind the wallflower plants.

Between the plants and the brick wall of the cottage it scampered, until it reached the foot of the rosebush, where it stopped abruptly. Far, far above it, lights glowed from the windows.

A tremor shook its tiny frame. Its nose and whiskers quivered at the sense of danger, and it turned to double back on its tracks, away from the half-remembered terrors of an alien world.

It hurried out into the moonlight and made for the open field beyond the hawthorn hedge. There among the rimy grass and the sweet familiar scents, its panic subsided.

Nibbling busily, safely within darting distance of its hole, the Christmas mouse was at peace with its little world.